THE
MEMORY
OF
SCENT

THE
MEMORY
OF
SCENT

LISA BURKITT

For Charlie and for Neil and Ethan

First published 2012

The History Press Ireland
119 Lower Baggot Street
Dublin 2
Ireland

www.thehistorypress.ie

© Lisa Burkitt, 2012

British Library Cataloguing in Publication Data.
A catalogue record for this book is available from the British Library.

ISBN 978 1 84588 738 4

Typesetting and origination by The History Press

WOODY ORIENTAL

The scent is patchouli. It took me a while to place it. Her
head must also lean against this very cushion, must also
watch as the painter strokes and separates the bristles of his
brushes and runs his thumb through them one by one. My
mother always wafted lavender. Her friends moved in drifts
of irises and violets. But here, propped up against this prickly,
horse-hair stuffed cushion, I can smell only patchouli.

Its mustiness coils through my nostrils and makes me
think of old, battered leather or something woody like over-
turned earth or the damp carpet of a forest after a spring
shower, at first lush and seductive, then sweetly stabbing like
walking barefoot on moss. It clouds behind my eyes until the
sound of the painter crossing the parquet floor is nothing but
a soft shuffle. I try not to clench my toes, because he likes me
looking wistful and sensuous. 'Like a Venus sprite', he said.
I don't know what he means. My nakedness is a lumpen and
mottled sheath, struggling to distinguish itself from the col-

ours and textures around me. That small stove is not enough to heat this large vaulted space. I need to channel a Venus sprite, to somehow inhabit her, but my veins are throbbing like angry blue rivers and my pimpled flesh should be slapped on to a butcher's counter ready for cleaving and not presented in a gilt-edged frame.

I am sure she knows instinctively how a Venus sprite should appear to him. I imagine, with her everything is delicate and nubile. Her hair probably naturally fans out on the pillow like silken rivulets. My frizzy tufts could instead be used to stuff this pillow that has been so heavily indented by my head. She passed close by on a few occasions. I knew it was her by her scent. And once, I held the door open for her as she made her way down the stairs just as I was arriving. I saw the buffed lace boots clip lightly down toward me, then the swish of the green velvet hem and the white scalloped underskirt as they grazed each step. Next the narrow leather belt and cinched-in waist came into view. As she neared the bottom, she adjusted her velvet hat with its little decorative bird peeping out from some netting, all fastened loosely at an angle under her chin in a thick ribbon. Her skin looked fresh and pink, her loose hair the blackest black under her broad-rimmed green velvet hat. As she passed through the doorway she dropped one of the white gloves she was pulling on. We both bent to pick it up at the same time. We smiled shyly. I could see why he would want to paint her. Her violet eyes would be just the kind of detail that a painter would get excited about. She walked as if bathed in a shimmer, while the beam of sunlight seemed only to amplify my blandness.

I have spent hours in this bare studio. Several of the canvases leaning against the wall remain blank and virginal, primed for the first lacerations of colour which he will build on stroke by stroke, curve by curve, nurturing and attentive until she is staring defiantly out at you, perhaps seductively, daring you to look for longer. Others are in rows against the wall and are a constant source of anxiety to me as I compare myself to the tangles of peach limbs, cascading hair and the coy over-the-shoulder glances.

I have to remind myself that he did choose me from among all those at the models' market in Place Pigalle. Sunday after Sunday, I stamped my feet trying to keep warm, while I milled around with young laundry girls in grey muslin, all praying for a sitting, for a few francs, for the next meal, all standing for hours on end while newly urbanised painters weaved around us in search of alabaster. They were met instead with reddened skin, chapped hands and untamed hair. Where did he find her I wonder?

'Fleur, drop that right shoulder just a little. The right shoulder', he says, as if I'm just a collection of body parts.

My mother never actually told me why she named me Fleur, but I know that it was in the expectation that I would live a life of fragrant gracefulness. There were always flowers freshly picked and bunched in surprising places around the house. Her needlework was exquisite, her deportment refined. I took on the awkward gait of my father, probably out of mimicry, because I adored him so. He also gifted me with the unfortunate thicker wrists and ankles more becoming of a son.

I wonder does the patchouli girl open her thighs for him, this man who is only referred to as the 'Spanish painter'. He does not look at me with any urgency, any tension. The patchouli is still strong, so maybe he is satiated. She cannot be long gone. Shafts of light peep through the olive-green shutters and lance little specks of dust. There is a plate of discarded bread and cheese and an almost empty bottle of red wine abandoned on a long, low wooden bench. There are two stained glasses on the floor and one chair. Did he straddle the bench while she sat on the chair? Did he take the glass from her before placing it on the floor? Did he turn towards her, his hands tracing her ankles then slowly hiking the gathered layers until he reached the top of her stockings? Did he begin to gently roll, downwards, silk tipped fingers …

'… and then that will be sufficient.'

'Pardon, Monsieur?'

'Next Thursday afternoon. If I need you then after that, I will ask you. Are you still at Café Guerbois?'

He has finished with me. One more session. How did my friend Maria beguile a man forty years her senior so completely that he now pays a regular stipend to her, even though he no longer paints her? She never spoke of lovemaking, nor did I ever press her for the no doubt unpalatable details of his crêpe skin and angular bones covering her and prodding her. It would be like a crow alighting on a field of strawberries. She only ever spoke of the grandeur of his Neuilly studio. Hers is a stubbornness that defies convention; she sees no reason why she should not be as great a painter as any man.

I am dispatched. I slowly pad my way to the oriental screen and, even though I boldly turn to face him, he has already begun to divide his brushes into the different jars according to the thickness of their bristles. I slip on my chemise and tighten my corset so that my apron looks trim on me. My petticoat could do with some starch and I may as well not have bothered wearing my favourite puff-sleeved blouse for all the attention it garnered. To think I spent wasted moments wondering: broach or cravat, cravat or broach. To think I generously tipped the long glass neck of my mother's jasmine scent on to my fingertips to dab some allure behind my ears and on to my neck. I don't have too great a choice when it comes to skirts, though I am straining at the fastenings of this one. My mother can let it out again. I can see him through the hinges of the screen, removing his paint-spattered smock as I bend to pull up my stockings. I lace up my boots and drape my shawl over my shoulders.

'I'll be leaving now.' But he waves indifferently over his shoulder without even rotating himself fully towards me. The steps are pockmarked from scores of women clicking their way up and down this stairwell. Some of the steps are so badly scuffed that you could trip quite easily if you were inattentive or distracted. I need both of my hands to pull open the front door and the lion's head seems to wink at me as the sunlight catches its brass. I fall into the bustle of these narrow streets, treading carefully around clumps of horse manure and rotting slimy vegetables. Weaving through the street stalls, I have to hitch up my skirt or else the putrid-smelling seepage coursing down the cobbles would leech into my hems. I am aware that the lace of my boot is dragging along the ground but I don't want to grab its sodden tip with an ungloved hand, so I ignore it. Gradually the grim littered doorways become fewer, the streets become wider, the strolling ladies better groomed and soon I am rounding the corner on to Rue Batignolles where the familiar row of canopies bulge and billow into view. I wave to the shop boy at the front of the colour merchant's store as he sweeps its entrance clean.

'You're late.' The *patron* of the café is angry with me.

'Mademoiselle, I am getting tired of your excuses and your absences and your disappearances. There are a dozen other girls I could hire like that.' He clicks his tobacco-stained fingers for emphasis. I know that he is right. I see them – young girls, perfectly pleasant and polite, knocking at the back door, asking to speak with him. But he likes me, and the customers seem to as well, and when I am here, I do work very, very hard – most of the time.

The *patron* has been in a bad mood since his wife left him for a clerk, a strange sullen man whose merits are mysterious. He seems to cast his own brooding shadow no matter how luminous the daylight. But many times, on the pretence of visiting her husband at his work, the *patron*'s wife would brush past the clerk's table and linger with her back to him. An odd habit I always thought, until I caught a glimpse of his hands on her hips beneath her shawl, tugging her gently towards him. He briefly nuzzled his head towards the small of her back, one florid cheek resting on her bustle. It was why he always chose to sit in the far booth. These furtive cameos play out with the randomness of paint splattering. One vast moving canvas, these walls its frame.

Walrus had his own reasons for sitting with his back to everyone.

'Psst … you're late!'

I normally don't mind being late, though I feign distress about it for the *patron*. But I do hate when I'm late and am immediately thrown into a flurry of busyness. Today is such a day. The café is filled with stragglers from the luncheon service, their hats still balancing on the wall hooks where they were tossed several hours earlier. Others are arriving in small groups, flicking up their frock coats to better arrange themselves on the metal chairs and around the small marble-topped tables. I stand in the middle and tie my apron at my waist as customers brush by me. With one extended sweep, I wipe a cloth over the bar counter which stretches along one wall of the café. I then bring my cloth over to the wood panelled booth where Walrus likes to sit, his thick arching moustache quivering at a point beneath his chin as he mocks my tardiness.

'What was it this time? You saved a duck from being bashed on the head by a boatman's pole?'

'You, Sir, given the chance, would have deliberately bashed it in, only to serve it up on a platter. No, I had a sitting.'

'Did you manage to prise his Catalonian fingers from his brushes long enough to stroke the back of your neck?'

Much to my annoyance, I feel my face flush. 'No, of course not. Nothing would have interested me less.'

He is not the slightest bit convinced. He settles his large rear in café after café and restaurant after restaurant, ostensibly out of his love of food, but it is more because he is a gourmand of life, greedily ingesting all round him. He lives vicariously through observation and can unpick the pretences and restraints that people swathe themselves in for the sake of social order. With one raised eyebrow, he can shatter any carefully constructed tableau and cut straight to its sweaty underbelly.

'Mademoiselle, you are annoyed that the handsome man from Catalan had reduced you to nothing more than brush strokes. You feel you could just as easily be a vase or a bowl of fruit, but you must know that a model is a mere vessel, nothing more. You can't blame the artist for that.'

'Yes, but when your toes and fingers are freezing and your skin has turned a shade of blue, don't you think the painter should at least notice ... should remember you are human and care just a little? Unless he wants to make love to you of course, yes, then he'll recall you are flesh and blood and not just some ... what did you call it? ... some vessel.'

'But he didn't want to make love to you, am I right? And that my young lady, if I am not mistaken, is the source of your irritation. You are insulted that he didn't even give you the right to refuse him.'

I snort slightly; an entirely affected attempt at being dismissive. Walrus taps his podgy hand on mine as I stack his plates with renewed efficiency.

'Mademoiselle, I know for a fact that he is not a nice man. That young girl who was found dead in the alleyway just off Rue Notre Dame des Champs, she kept regular company with him. Granted, that street contains more studios than any street in Paris, but he did take her in. They were then evicted from their apartment because no rent was being paid. He just left her to fend for herself. She was a rural girl whose only real possession was her coat. She pawned it and died on the streets, probably of exposure. There were bruises on her body.'

Walrus is speaking quickly and in hushed tones so that I won't appear to be dawdling during a busy service. Stories of lost girls are nothing new. It's a sad world. I know that from my early days here. Walrus can be very dramatic. It keeps him from being bored. I can hear *chef* calling me from the kitchen. Walrus pats his moustache with a napkin, lifts his hat from the wall, and hefts his way out through and around the other customers. I know that by the time he reaches the front step, several small objects will have teetered and crashed to the floor. I go to fetch a small brush.

The Café Guerbois has its own rhythms, from the light luncheon clatter to the more animated evening sessions when the air becomes thick with the smoke which curls high around the paintings hanging on the wood panels while the young *serveuses* dart around taking orders and serving drinks. Artists corral themselves into one section and hold charged discussions on painting styles and the best moment to varnish. Poets and students idle in dark corners with watered-down beers in contemplation of life. I like to soak up the streams of café conversations as I would spilt wine – a dab here, a trickle there. Poverty is a recurring theme. I quietly scorn their notion that the more poverty you endure, the more noble a life you live. I once heard them speak in awe of an old friend who wrote 'An Ode to Poverty', and then died of starvation. So many of them spend all their time drinking on credit and avoiding actual work. Men do not realise what a rarefied life they lead in their industrious pursuit of leisure. Women must remain busy or all around them would crumble.

And here is George. There is something intriguing about him, from the way his long fingers tap the stem of his goblet to the way he smells, which is a mixture of lavender cologne and tobacco. He is almost as handsome as the Spaniard and has the casual air of entitlement that comes from being adored all of his life by governesses, elderly aunts, and a besotted mother, an endless parade of validation for his every utterance, his every bowel movement. I have learned that he dropped out of school before completing his *Baccalauréat* because he was fixated on becoming a painter. To the general agreement of those present, by even the loosest of standards, he was never going to be any good. So he turned to writing, at which he seems much more comfortable. He managed to get an essay published to much back-slapping relief.

I want to dislike him for his ease of passage through life, but he is unfailingly polite and respectful. He once even half stood up while I delivered his food to the table, before he realised what he was doing and sat back down, as was completely appropriate to our relative positions.

Circumstances shape people and some are more blessed than others. I try not to let my annoyance become too obvious that this world in which I am now anchored, through which I am dragging myself with cracked and dirty fingernails, is a mere source of adventure and new impressions for unmotivated students and untalented artists and writers. That really my friends and I are just bit parts in the fanciful montage of young men who come to Paris to earn their stripes and then be gone.

Where has the time gone? The hour of the 'Green Fairy' is soon here, and I must lay out more sugar cubes. If I was blindfolded, I could tell you the time of day it was simply by raising my nose in the air and sniffing. Mornings have the sizzling, buttery comfort of frying eggs; late mornings start to choke up with pungent cigarettes and coffee; then, my favourite, the steaming wafts of soup; before the dreaded hour where absinthe is ordered in enthusiastic rounds and then slowly, you can actually witness a palpable descent into sadness.

You see, here we are a safe-house from the visceral, gut punch of rejection by dealers, lovers, friends, publishers. Some handle it with table-thumping bravado and another round of vermouth, but the absinthe gently finger-tips others towards the edge. They think they are being soothed but as I serve up yet another glass of the iced, opal-green elixir, their shoulders slump a little further, their breathing sinks a little deeper, their eyes take on the flinty glaze of the browbeaten. Within a few hours, their demolition will be complete.

Today I will take my time walking home. I am tired and limp and these streets act like bellows, pumping vitality back into my lungs. I love the brutish pursuit of the aesthetic that is typical of Paris. To think that an administrator with

Napoleonic ties could just decide, for the sake of the prom-
enading upper middle class, to cut though and obliterate
what was once a chaotic mess of narrow streets and trans-
form them into great tree-lined avenues. People can now
stroll to see and be seen. To then demolish medieval streets
and alleys so that the noses of the better classes could be
spared the stench of their foul-smelling subordinates? I can
understand it. Why would you not want to annihilate things
that are messy, smelly and complex and replace them instead
with simplicity and refinement?

But here, as I begin to thread my way through the rabbit-
warren of dirty streets which lead to my own front door
at the top of Montmartre, my breathing becomes easier. It's
strange, as much as I love the scale and grandeur of the finer
parts of the city, it is in Montmartre I find my comfort.

And of course, there's young Joseph in his threadbare, old
man's coat. He is collecting horse dung. He balances his large
basket on his hip and scoops up his 'investment' which he
will later mix with straw and sell on to fertilise the finer gardens. He has been doing this since he was five years of age.
The two prostitutes who have taken him in regularly take
turns flinging buckets of cold water on him after his hard
day's work because of the stink. He can be heard cursing at
them. He is a young man of twelve years of age now and is
more precious about his nakedness than he used to be. I have
tried to teach him to read, just a little, and he does, just a little.

'*Maman*, I'm home.'

I go straight over to the small grate to poke the fire, trying
to keep it spitting warmth, but its crackle is that of a winded
old man. I feel overwhelmed with tenderness for my mother
and I'm consumed by a ferocious urge to protect her. Our
home is a jumble of rickety cast-off furnishings, shreds of

matting on the bare floors, sagging mattresses and one large cracked mirror. Can lodgings ever really be considered home? My early days were spent in a place with climbing roses over a front door, with a parlour and proper bedrooms, a large kitchen and a laundry and a pantry. Here in this converted outbuilding, where our ceiling is somebody else's floor and the chairs of upstairs lives can be heard scraping above us, I have two carefully placed, red velvet cushions. I plump them each morning and prop them against the frayed arms of the sofa. My pride is something sheathed and stitched in dimpled red velvet and delicately positioned for inspection. It is evident in few other places.

Though her fingers are pale and stiffening, my mother continues to sew with her sewing box resting on the blanket on her knees. She mends table linen for a few restaurants and hotels, making the threadbare look refined. It brings in a little money.

'No word from Rue de la Paix yet then?'

'None, *Maman*. I'm sure any day now, something will come up.'

When I picture Rue de la Paix in my mind I see one vast emporium of opulence. The very best milliners are concentrated on that one street. I have tried on many occasions to find my mother work there, but they prefer young girls, pretty girls, probably because the customers are free to wander about the shops, watching the girls at work. The idea seems to be that if you are trying to sell something well-crafted to a discerning customer, even the nimble-fingered hat maker has to be visually appealing. There are small and busy ateliers where the hats are crafted and assembled and there are vast parlours of indulgence where, when you step through the doors, you can feel the lush carpet through even the crudest of soles.

The hats there are so exquisite that they are displayed on tall bronze stands so you can perambulate around them, admiring the elaborate confections of ostrich plumes and feathers, silk trims and ribbons, felt, velvet and lace.

I once dreamt that I was a lady in the mood for a purchase, and was led to a wide, marble table where I sat on a cushioned chair in front of an enormous gold-gilded mirror. The air was perfumed with freshly cut flowers, and an offertory of hats was presented to me, one by one, by slimly elegant young ladies. As I sipped Champagne from a sparkling, crystal flute, I waved them all away with one imperious white-gloved hand. I could never find work for my mother in a place like that and, much to her irritation, I don't have my mother's fine skills with a needle nor the required patience.

My mother, the once elegant Madame Delphy, knows that I had mentioned the possibility of her working with some master milliners. Her thoughts have become frail and loose and she seems to have no perception of time at all. Time has become a fluid and itinerant thing that her mind randomly plucks at. She harvests her memories as she would apples in an orchard, scooping up the healthy fruit, while discarding the bruised and damaged. She knows that her husband, my father, is dead, but has forgotten that he died leaving colossal debt. She knows that she had loved him, but forgets that he often disappeared down to Marseille under the guise of his engineering work where he would take up with prostitutes and find willing players for high-stake card games. She knows that she often doesn't feel very well and that is the confusing thing for both of us as her mind and body seem in the interminable grip of a cloying melancholy. Sometimes she aimlessly picks at the wallpaper as she lies in her bed at night, creating a jagged gash that cruelly mocks me. 'Your mother is ill,' that wallpaper wound taunts me as the sun rises each day and blinks into darkness each night.

'Yoo-hoo, ladies of the house?'

Maria waves from outside the window before she bursts through the door carrying a small posy of flowers and some bread. 'These are for your mother.'

'Ah how sweet. Let me put them in water. She is a little tired so is having a rest. I'll make us some coffee.'

Maria pulls the chair that isn't broken, towards me and whispers so that we are not heard. 'How has she been?'

'Very confused. Sometimes she wakes me at night with her moaning and I find she's covered with sweat.'

The fact that we were both fatherless forged an immediate bond between Maria and I when we first met as young girls. However, while I have fond memories of a tall man tapping up the path with his silver-topped cane and then tossing his hat on to a bench, scooping me up, all in a tobacco-scented whirl, there was nothing for Maria. She would joke that she was, 'Marie-Clémentine Valadon, Father-Unknown', because that's what is written on her birth certificate. Maria is fingering the wide blue ribbon of her bonnet.

'Another new hat, Maria?'

'It's Henri. He spends far too much time going in and out of the milliners picking up hats for me. I tell him that it's much cheaper to paint me in the nude, instead of in these creations. But what can I do?' Her smile tells me that she wouldn't be protesting too much about this.

'Yesterday we went to that lovely wild garden behind the Boulevard de Clichy with the lemon trees and the lilac bushes. It was a slow day's work, some painting, a little wine and pâté, and then more painting in that very crisp, sharp light. You didn't make the party last night?'

'I hadn't the energy, so I just stayed home after work. How was it?'

'The usual: noisy and lots of fun. It was in one of the dilapidated streets near the Louvre. Somebody painted three large banners with the words, 'obligation', 'order' and 'responsibility' in big dark letters. They were hung on the wall and the men had a spitting competition to find out how many of the banners they could hit. Heads flung back, and then 'phwat'. There was one poor soul, a small timid writer who didn't manage to reach any of them, so he was tumbled out onto the street where he was pelted with tomatoes and everyone shouted 'traitor' after him. Henri and I stayed far too late, of course.'

Henri is a bit of a night owl. I like him. I think his insecurities make him comfortable to be around and he is instantly recognisable, a little bearded man with the bulbous nose and checked trousers. He adores Maria, which is probably why he paints her so much. 'Henri de Toulouse-Lautrec'. His name has the ring of the nobility which he does indeed spring from, but I would say he is more at home among the girls of Montmartre. They all love him because he is the first with the gossip.

'Did he hear anything about the girl in the alley, the one that was found dead? Walrus was talking about her earlier.'

'Well, he didn't know her. Very few did. She was often with that Spanish painter. I heard that she had pawned her coat so he went to the pawn shop to get it back after she was found, and then he and a few friends went to the Jardin des Tuileries to hold a farewell ceremony for the girl. They placed her coat on the ground, sprinkled petals on it, and set it on fire. They called it a ceremony of release and drank until dawn.'

'They probably didn't even remember her name by then.' I can, in a way, see how he would easily show such a callous disregard for a young girl. But actual cruelty? That I can't imagine. And yet, why couldn't he have retrieved her coat for her while she was still alive? No doubt he would have if she had only asked. I'll hold that thought.

'Maria, I sat for him, the Spaniard, and he was absolutely fine. In fact I have another sitting next week.' Or was he fine? When I think about it, there were moments where I felt a little frightened, but only because I was so anxious to please him and felt as though I was falling short. Being so talented must be a very consuming business and from such talented people we can't expect the social niceties beloved of the terminally boring and vacuous. And then there was the cat. It innocently strolled in one afternoon, back arched in anticipation of exploring a new environment. Any distraction can be welcome when you are holding the same position for hours on end. He caught the side glance that was really just a reflex, and swung around to see the source of my brief flickering of focus. The cat purred its entitlement to be there and padded towards one of the jars of brushes sitting on the floor. With the palette firmly wedded to his left hand, he reached for the cat with his right hand and closed his fist around its neck, carrying it swinging and spitting to the top of the stairs. He must have flung it down because I could hear a few thuds and pitiful mewing. It actually didn't take anything out of him as he just slowly closed the door and resumed painting. I was almost afraid to breathe. How safe was I really? What about the patchouli girl … is she safe?

* * *

The air always seems fresher here in the Bois de Boulogne than in most other parts of Paris, apart, of course, from the clean air of the Butte at the height of Montmartre. I have been promising Maria that I would come with her out here to the circus where once she spent time as an acrobat. She has left many old friends behind and the odd time I take a day trip out here, there seems to be a certain grace, a casual respectability where ladies with parasols and impeccable men with their walking sticks mingle and casually appraise the red-coated riders as they canter their horses through complicated routines. We pick our way behind the tiered stands, trying to avoid the still steaming clumps of horse manure. Maria looks sublimely happy, as if caught up in a mystical thrall.

'Is that not the most wonderful smell in the entire world?' I smile meekly because my only concern is to swat away the flies and to try and ignore the discomfort I am feeling as sullen groups of men work in industrious hives, some pulling ropes, others painting large planks of wood, while all around, calloused hands savagely groom glossy horse flesh with coarse bristled brushes.

'Uncle.' I turn in time to see Maria clasping her hat to her head and running towards a large man perched on a very small wooden stool and tending to a horse's hoof. I watch, charmed, as a broad grin creases his weather-worn face the minute he realises it is Maria. He releases the horse's hoof from between his knees and stands up, his bulky, scarred forearms gripping Maria in the briefest of hugs. This man, whom one second ago I looked on with misgivings and suspicion, tentatively stepping around him as if proximity would bring me harm, is now bathed in benevolence and awkward charm.

'My little Marie-Clémentine, look at you. You don't look like a girl who has come to do some tumbling.'

'This is my good friend Fleur, and this is my uncle.'

I know he is not really her uncle, but she always speaks so fondly of him because he took care of her. Everyone should have at least one person to look out for them.

'This little creature was the most fearless acrobat ever to climb up on a horse's back. There were plenty bigger, but none bolder. And your trapeze work …'

'Yes, well, my boldness cost me months in bed and my future in the circus.'

'Oh that was a nasty fall you took, but look at you now, haven't you grown into the proper young lady.'

I am intruding on this affectionate reunion so I decide to take a look around. I don't even like circuses. They always seem pompous and artificial and I hate being condescended to, all that manipulation of the audiences' reactions. All that, 'Oooooh, he almost fell to his death there.' 'Ahhhhh, that elephant nearly crushed his body there.' Leave me in peace to look at a painting, or walk in a beautiful garden, or eat an exquisitely cooked meal. I much prefer to be a passive observer, than a sawdust-caked participant.

Maria was very happy here so I am happy for her. As I stroll around, I can see how a very strong bond would form between all those involved in this little capsule of existence. They must have to truly trust each other. They must learn to read each others rhythms when their very life could depend on something as tenuous as another's wrist clasp as they fly through the air. They must know what ropes to haul, what animals to soothe, what smiles to flash, what has to be hammered here and fastened there. It must all come as second nature, as intricate and tuned as the workings of a clock. There is a large trapeze net and a man springing up and down with a rope tied to his waist as two men each hold one end of it. I pull back a canvas flap as I can hear voices inside. It is a huge space with one long bar area where three young women dry glasses while others flatten out sand heaps underfoot. They barely look up at me, even though they must know, must sense, that I am not of this place. Back outside again, a strong man holds two women aloft, one in each arm. His muscles are slathered in something; his vanity is clearly outstripping the women's safety for I feel sure they will slide off the glistening and sinewy bulges. His manhood is tucked into folds of cloth, resembling something you would swaddle a baby in, his chest broad and bare.

I feel more inclined now to brazenly lift the various canvas flaps as if peeping through a picture book. There is a whimpering sound coming from somewhere. I slowly step my way towards the source of it, which appears to be behind a wooden screen. There, standing naked with little skinny arms crossed in front of her, is a young girl of about fourteen or fifteen, head bowed with her dark hair falling forward. A man is walking around her as if he is inspecting merchandise. I remember hearing recently that the circus owner likes to stage side-show cabarets for select bands of gentlemen where they are entertained by nude girls. I hear myself shouting.

'What the hell are you doing?'

The man's eyes meet mine with a steely gaze. 'And who, might I ask, are you?'

I am emboldened and move to grab the wrist of the young girl but an unkempt elderly woman sitting on a small stool in the shadows startles me as she presses down hard on her haunches and rears up like an angry beast.

'Leave my granddaughter alone. Don't you go near her.'

The woman has a walking stick, and she raises it to hit me but I step back. I feel contempt for this woman rising biliously from deep in my stomach. The man throws a blanket at the young girl.

'Look, the customers here are high class. This is not some brawling absinthe-soaked hovel. Anyway, I would never hire her: she is far too young and far too skinny. All of you just get out of here immediately and good riddance.' Then, with a swipe of his forearm, he bursts out through the flap and into the afternoon air. The young girl starts to cry.

'I am sorry, *grand-mère*.' She begins to dress herself with the weariness of an eighty-year-old. The woman turns to me with flinty eyes and hisses at me.

'Why would you do this? Who do you think you are?'

The woman suddenly slumps back on to her stool as if broken. She wipes her eyes, then stands up and limps over to the girl to help her dress. She tenderly smoothes out the girl's long hair.

'Don't worry sweetheart. Your *grand-mère* will find something.'

I slowly back away, knowing that neither the woman nor the girl would even notice. I ease my way out to look for Maria. I want to leave immediately.

* * *

Maria and I drag ourselves slowly up the steep incline of the Rue Lepic where she has arranged to meet Henri in the Bonne Franquette bar. It is painted in a dark green, and the shutters have faded to an anaemic grey. There is little about it that is warm and inviting but still, many trawl up the hill to slay their demons here and it somehow fits my mood at this moment.

'Ladies, here, try some of this. It will test you.' Henri pushes his glass across the table towards me and I take a quick sip, nearly spitting it out again.

'What is this devil's brew?'

'A wonderful mixture of absinthe, red wine and cognac,' he winks.

'I don't have your constitution. I'll have a cherry brandy please.'

Maria requests a small beer. Henri clicks for the attention of the server.

'Have you heard about the splattering?' Henri is now poised on the edge of his chair with his eyes glistening. 'Well, they are calling it that, which I think is most clever.'

I take a sip of this much more familiar drink and wait until he has exhausted his dramatic pause.

'A painter was found dead at his easel yesterday morning. One of his models found him slumped there and alerted the police. She came rushing out and bumped into a young laundry girl who also modelled for him and the laundry girl kept shouting, "but he owes me ten francs!"'

That seems bizarre, but also teasingly alluring as a topic of conversation over a warm cherry brandy. Henri is in his element.

'And who was the painter? The very same Spaniard that the dead girl was last seen with. So, poetic justice I would have to class that.'

My breathing is sucked into an involuntary spasm.

'The police have cordoned off the area and are already asking his associates about his movements and who he spent time with? They are also trying to find the model who discovered him because she seems to have disappeared, and you know what they say about the last person to have seen a murder victim?'

A shiver slithers down my spine. There are some very unsavoury drifters and all manner of low-lifes wandering about: thieves, addicts, pimps and often the most sordid among them gravitate towards each other. Instinctively they seek each other out, like lambs to a teat. Could it have been poetic justice? Did he get what was coming to him? I am aware that the fingernails of my right hand have drifted towards my teeth, and I am beginning to nip at them. It is a throwback to my childhood, a self-comforting reflex and I have to make a very big effort to force my hands back on to my lap. Who was the model? I am worried about the patchouli girl. I assume an air of casual intrigue so as not to sounds ridiculous.

'There is one of his models, I forget her name, that I would quite like to find. How do you think I should do it? How would you, Henri … do painters overlap on models?'

'Only the good ones. The good ones are like prizes. A beautiful model had been the severing of many a friendship. Is your friend beautiful?'

'Yes.'

'But you forget her name?'

'Well, I wasn't really that close to her, but I would really like to find her. I'm feeling concerned.'

'Fleur, you do know that Paris is a big place?'

'I heard the Spaniard tried to poach some of Auguste Renoir's models. Maybe she was one of them.'

I can see how this is going to unfold as Maria straightens herself on her chair. 'Well, he didn't try and poach me and I am one of Auguste's favourites at the moment.'

Henri is scowling. 'And don't forget that. It is only for the moment.'

Maria matches his scowl. 'He is a little in love with me.'

Henri makes a 'puh!' sound and lifts his glass to his fleshy lips. Henri and Maria gossip for another twenty minutes or so, as I try to indicate that I am ready to leave by shifting around in my chair. Maria eventually takes the hint. I link her arm as we step out of the Bonne Franquette and down on to the street. I am studying the way fresh dirt has caked the grooves of the cobblestones and wondering if it is possible to find a girl wearing patchouli in a city like Paris. I hear its faint buzzing and notice a wayward bee. I duck and spring and flap my arms because they terrify me, but fascinate me also. I remember my astonishment the first time I saw a bee here in Paris as I had always associated them with rural idylls and agricultural living, from everything to do with my life before. And there it was, insistently buzzing its incongruity. But why shouldn't they live in this great city, with the chestnut-tree-lined Champs-Élysées and the Tuilleries and the orchards of Montmartre? I understand those of the countryside appliquéing their way of life onto the fabric of this new urban world. I understand how so many rooftops were seen as ideal homes for bee hives. I understand how those people, my people, would startle at the rattle and clang of steam-cars and want to taste honey.

* * *

1 pair curtains (lace)
6 table cloths (linen)
Assorted serviettes

I check the items off against *Maman*'s scribbled list and bundle them up into one large strip of brown paper. Maria holds it all down while I tie it with string. I have been punctuating our conversation with references to the Spaniard's model and I want to find out more about the girls that Renoir would use.

'Fleur, I know for a fact that Auguste hasn't been using anyone else for quite some time now. We have just completed the dancing paintings. In fact, a jealous mistress barged into the studio and attacked me with a broom, because we had been spending such a long time together. Imagine! Mad whore. Chased me away as if I was a rat or something. Even if your friend did model for him, he may not know who she is. For Monsieur Auguste Renoir, women are really just a collection of different flesh tones and not much more.'

'But where does he start looking for his models? Do they go to him?'

'You really do want to find this girl?'

Maria rummages through some scraps of paper on *Maman*'s sewing table and reaches for a pencil. She starts to sketch out the head of a young woman.

'Can you describe her for me?'

I close my eyes and of course, the overwhelming sensation is one of smell. I concentrate, and the beautiful face with its quick dimpled flash of a smile, looms immediately into my mind. Maria sketches as the details tumble out.

'Her lips are a little fuller, the chin a little smaller.'

She shades and darkens and rubs with her fingers. The face emerging from the scrap of paper is close to what I remember.

'I am making her look a little like you.'

'My God no, this girl is beautiful … make her hair longer and her eyes wider. You can draw me another time.'

I have seen some of Maria's sketches before, of herself, of her mother, of everyday objects, little pencil and charcoal drawings, but I have never watched as a few light lines stutter and shift into a recognisable image. It is truly a talent.

'Fleur, we can go by Rue d'Orchampt to see if Auguste is at his studio today, and you can show this drawing around in case anyone else recognises this girl.'

'Good. We'll do that on the way to Agnes's café with *Maman*'s linen.'

I carefully tie up one large bundle in brown paper and string. I knot my hair and tuck it into my straw hat. I fold Maria's drawing and put it into my skirt pocket. We make our way down the hill passing the dance halls which will remain shut and sullen until five o'clock this evening before bursting open in a heady glow of excitement. Horse-drawn carriages clatter by, forcing us to jump to one side. And unfortunately, here comes our village idiot, bless him, old Edmond limping furiously towards us. He is known around here as 'the windmill', because he has no control over his right arm which constantly flails about. He also drags his left leg. He shoves a cracked tin daguerreotype into our faces of a handsome dark-haired young man with a steady gaze wearing a heavy coat. His elbow is resting on a shelf or table and his long fingers are clasped in front of him. 'Have you seen my son?'

'No, Edmond, not today', we both coo reassurance. He then moves on to another man who has overtaken us at a quick pace. With the same aggressive gesture, he pushes the image towards his face, causing the man to step back and lose his balance, falling in a heap on the ground. Standing over him, he again shouts, 'Have you see my son?' before limping on. Maria and I rush to help the man on to his feet.

'Are you all right?'

'He's insane.' We look at each other mid-hoist. This man is clearly not at all sympathetic as he angrily dusts off the sleeves of his frock coat.

'Well, he is actually. Poor Edmond lost his son at the barricades during the siege eleven years ago.'

'Look at my coat.'

I am aware that Maria is beginning to square up to him, so I intervene.

'His mind is gone. He was fighting along with his son, and the boy was shot in the head in front of him. Even though his brains were splattered on his coat, he couldn't take it in.'

'Ah yes, the glorious six-week siege. Well, if stories are to be believed, men ran bare-chested into hails of bullets.'

Now I am annoyed. 'Yes, *Monsieur*, it was a glorious time, where briefly the working class and middle class came together in a common cause.'

'Briefly indeed, young lady. Those of any wisdom, and may I say distinction, did the sensible thing and fled Paris for Versailles and elsewhere, tiring very quickly of all that wine-shop posturing. There was nothing noble about that uprising: twenty-five-thousand dead and all because of class hatred. That communard idiot who just assaulted me probably listened to too many bad writers and mediocre painters trumpeting their intellectual and moral degeneracy with a cheap beer in one hand and a bad speech in the other. Ladies, I wish you good day.'

We watch stunned as the stranger marches off and I am furious that I lacked his eloquence, for I wanted to shut him up, to fell him verbally with something incisive.

'Damned tourists', Maria sighs after a long pause and we both laugh because it is such a pathetic and belated rejoinder. I just had a horrible thought; that could be me years from now, waving my arms about and shoving Maria's little sketch of my patchouli girl into the faces of perfect strangers. In years to come when they talk about the windmills of Montmartre, they could be talking about me and Edmond. We walk on.

'This is silly. I'm sure she's perfectly fine. She'll be having all sorts of adventures to tell her grandchildren about.'

'Your model? Are you sure?'

'Of course. She is none of my business. Walrus says I have to stop befriending stray people.'

'Good. Then if I said to you there's Auguste's bicycle leaning up against Julien Tanguy's shop, you wouldn't be interested?'

'Is it?'

'Definitely. He must be in buying some paints.'

I think about it only briefly and feel a flutter of excitement as I will hear for the first time how it will sound to verbalise this desperate and illogical hunt for a girl I know chiefly by scent. I hand my parcel to Maria. On second thoughts, I take it from her again, and nudge her in the back to go in first. She is the one who knows him after all. A small bell tinkles as the door opens up into the narrow shop. There are rows and rows of paintings hanging alongside and above and below each other, reaching high up to the ceiling, crowding every inch of the walls. There is a deep wooden counter and on the far side of it, the owner, Père Tanguy, is cutting into a large roll of canvas.

'*Bonjour, Mesdemoiselles.* I'll be with you in a second.'

'No, it's Monsieur Renoir I wanted a quick word with.' I shuffle forward as I say this. The painter is holding the canvas taut along the counter to allow for ease of cutting. He turns towards me and swiftly appraises me from head to toe, one sweeping glance taking in the length of my body. He simply smiles and says; 'Yes, mademoiselle?' He is a handsome man, though his beard is not as full as I like to see on a man. Fullness seems to me to indicate virility. His is a little on the thin side, though I know his conquests are many, and that they include Maria, whom he now notices.

'Ah, my little acrobat, what brings you here?' He has let go of the canvas, much to Père Tanguy's annoyance as it springs back over his cutting hand. Maria stands with her hands behind her back and sways slightly, as a little girl does in anticipation of some ice cream. She says nothing, just smiles a smile I'm sure he has often been thrown. It says, 'I know your secrets; I know what you really like. I have brought you to your knees.' I hand Maria my parcel and take her sketch from my pocket to show to him.

'Monsieur, I am trying to find somebody. She is a model, long black hair, slim with violet eyes. Has she ever modelled for you or do you know of her? She sat recently for the Spanish painter.'

Renoir takes my sketch but doesn't yet look at it. He plucks at his lips.

'That Spaniard. I'm sure the last time I saw him was in here.'

Père Tanguy looks up. 'Vermilion and burnt umber. You were low on both.'

'Of course.' He now looks at the sketch while I continue.

'I'm trying to find this girl, and I thought maybe you may have used her at some point.'

'Never liked that Spaniard. Didn't know much about him except that he had a bit of a reputation as a scoundrel and scrounger. He'll pull up a chair beside you at the Nouvelles-Athènes, and manage to drink all night without dipping in his own pocket once. Do you know him, Julien?'

'He sounds like someone I would make pay up front.' He looked again at the sketch. 'No, the description is not familiar to me.'

I feel deflated and thank both gentlemen for their time while I reach for the latch of the door.

'Nice little sketch there.'

Maria steps forward. 'Thank you Monsieur Renoir. That would be mine. And if you'd like to buy me some tubes, I would be happy to paint it for you. It has been suggested to me that I change my name to "Suzanne". Do you think that would suit me – "Suzanne Valadon"? She is a figure in literature who keeps older men in thrall apparently.'

I try to steer 'Suzanne' towards the door. She has clearly not forgiven Renoir his angry mistress. We tumble out onto the street and walk past the Crémerie, where occasionally we treat ourselves to a nice afternoon coffee and some cakes. And why shouldn't we? Women of every class like to eat cake. I am thankful that I am unable to afford these sweet diversions more often that I do, as the band of my skirt leaves a red indent on my midriff, warning me each night as I undress for bed, that the slimness of my younger days will soon be a distant memory. The pink welt is like some horrible precursor to a slovenly middle age where the corsets become more restrictive and the attempted allure becomes something you can only snatch at with little, constrained breaths in case you faint, or explode. I'll be fortunate if I can get into my twenties without having to add some more side fastenings.

I am in the habit of watching the way other women carry themselves and, extraordinarily, age has little to do with magnetism. I observe the way men glance as if their heads have been yanked by an invisible string when certain women walk by. They could be walking with their wives and children and still that string will tug. I am more intrigued by what it is about the woman to cause this tug, what connects that string to her, as it is not always evident to me. Is it in the carriage? The swing of the hips? The toss of hair? Agnes is one such woman and we are now here at her strange little café. No tin-top tables here, her café has a shabby elegance, not unlike herself. Though now slightly stouter in appearance, she has the dignified deportment and captivating profile that so many artists have scrambled to paint over the past two decades. Her long grey-flecked hair still has a tint of its former auburn glory. The eyes remain the blue pools of mischievousness that have lured many to her bed.

'Fleur, my darling, come into the back so I can inspect your mother's handiwork. And Maria, here take this wine and glasses and find us a nice quiet corner. Look, that small table over there.'

'Of course.'

Agnes pulls back a curtain leading into the kitchen and, placing my parcel on a long wooden table, she unties the string. She picks through each item, carefully studying corners and hems and happily declares everything to be up to its usual standard.

'Now! Refreshments!' She grabs a plate of cheese and tears off some bread and we sit down beside Maria.

'*Salut*. Now, my lovelies, some gossip please. On whose canvases can we view your peachy little bottoms these days?'

'I did have some work, only the painter dropped dead. Maria is keeping Henri busy.'

'Oh, of course, the Spaniard. What a mystery. Did he drop dead or was there anything more sordid afoot? It's all very intriguing. It makes a welcome change from the boring speculation that passes for conversation around here at the moment. It's all about jockeying to be represented in the new independent *salon*. Did either of you get to that exhibition in the Tuileries Garden? It was so disorganised; held in what was just a huge wooden shed. And, oh, the squabbling and jealousy that has been breaking out here lately. All too full of their own importance. Enough of them. Who is kicking their legs too high at the Moulin de la Galette these days? If only I could cartwheel across a floor the way I used to.'

'Fleur is on a mission.' Maria appears hugely amused and is making fun of me a little. Nonetheless, I take her sketch out and show it to Agnes.

'I'm not sure if you could call it a mission, but have you seen a young model who looks a little like this, Agnes? I came across her modelling for the Spaniard, and one of his models found him and is now being sought by the police. It is a slim chance that she could have fallen into some difficulty.'

I would like to pretend that there is a strong bond of sisterhood amongst all the models, those of us at the lower echelons of life, those of us who at times feel low enough to consider allowing any man with a few francs to lift our skirts in a back alley for a few fevered seconds of grunting and a slimy discharge. But in truth, each is highly protective of her own patch. Each is one gutter away from oblivion. Agnes tenderly holds the sketch in both hands as she strokes it with one of her thumbs. To our surprise, tears spring to her eyes.

'How sweet. Just look at her.' She stares hard at me. 'This young model could be any young model.'

She places it on the table and slides it back over to me. She pours some more wine and lifts the corner of her white apron to dab at her eyes. We are unsure what to say next.

'Do you know her?' I ask in both dread and hope. The garrulous hostess and larger-than-life Agnes, now needs a few moments of stillness to compose herself. I bite my lip in anxiety at Agnes's discomfort. Agnes sniffs into her hankie.

'No, I don't think so. But these young girls can be so inno-cent. They can be so taken in by some of these painters who use them up, then toss them aside like a turpentine-soaked rag. Of course there can be the odd genuine love story, but very rarely do they survive the scrutiny of class or the novelty of fresh flesh. A differently shaped thigh, a new cascade of tumbling curls.'

I am disappointed and Agnes is misty eyed, becoming lost in recollection. I am irrelevant at this point.

'You know my mother was very pretty with fine features and fair hair. She was a noted beauty. She could pose as if a countess or a street girl. When my father chose her to model, she didn't mind the hours of cold and boredom because she knew that they would then go for a stroll and find a warm café, drink wine and talk for hours. She would visit his little apartment and pick his clothes off the floor and tidy away his books and papers. On Sundays they would take a picnic basket and find a pleasant river-view spot to idle and eat while watching the sailing boats and rowing skiffs.'

'They must have been madly in love.' Maria is becoming enthralled.

'I think they were, for a while. But it was when my mother was pregnant with me, that Papa started looking around for other models. The one he settled most quickly on was a very young red-haired Irish girl. I was told that my mother immediately hated her.' Agnes laughs a little, then goes over to a high shelf and reaches for another bottle of wine which she opens and slowly pours.

'My mother had to watch as Papa slowly became besotted with this new girl. This girl, Josie – the name is seared in my brain – her father was an aspiring writer and a drunk, and he had dragged the young girl to Paris. From what I understand, she seemed to have a delicacy that drove my father wild in his need to be protective of her. His best friend told me that he painted feverish portraits of her for hours on end then would bring her outside for fresh air and they would visit different cafés. He probably just wanted to show her off. Can you imagine how my mother was feeling at this stage?'

Agnes begins to laugh again, but it is a hollow sound. 'It backfired though, because on one of their excursions, a painter of much greater renown than my father approached Josie to see if she would pose for him. She readily agreed and became less available to Papa. So of course, he begins to lose interest in his own work and instead became obsessed with how "'his" Josie was being portrayed by his rival. She stopped sitting for my father entirely, as his jealousy turned him into an unrecognisable brute and she became afraid of him. Even though I was still a very small child and needed to be fed and cared for, it was said that my father would spend days creeping around outside the art studio on Rue Hautefeuille where Josie spent long hours posing. He would peer through the window and was almost driven demented when she started to pose nude. He would stomp around his studio, complaining to the few friends that he had left, that the paintings were becoming too erotic. He was fixated by how the light caught her breasts, how her white hand rested on her pubic hair, how small and delicate her bare feet looked as she lay there.'

'Your poor mother. How did she live with that?' At least my own mother was protected from the reality of my father's Marseille trips. She still had her pride, even if it was an illusion.

'Well, I can only vaguely remember the afternoon my mother smashed a vase of flowers on the floor.'

Agnes takes a deep drink from her glass as she drifts back into her childhood, summoning up the details. 'I remember they were pretty flowers that my mother had picked especially. I remember the smell of cooking and her checking herself in the mirror and fixing her hair as she heard Papa's heavy footfall on the stairs. I remember her sad smile as she stood by the neatly set table. I was in a pretty new dress. I remember being confused as the smile faded when my father just took his boots off and went into the bedroom slamming the door after him without saying a word. *Maman* grabbed the vase, stormed into the bedroom and screamed as she shattered the vase into little pieces against the bedstead. She untied her apron and kept saying over and over, "I can't go on. I can't go on."'

Agnes seems draped in sadness. 'I tried to keep up with Mama through the narrow streets. I hadn't learned how to button up my shoes yet, you see, so one of them fell off. "*Maman*, my shoe." But my mother just kept walking. I began to cry. My foot was bleeding by the time Mama stopped at the river's edge. "Such pretty sailing boats." I remember that was the last thing she said.'

After a long moment Agnes inhales deeply. 'Her body was retrieved further along the Seine about three days later.' An aching stillness hangs in the air.

'And your father?' Maria stutters.

'You know, in a strange way, he seemed less agitated after my mother's death. It was as if he had unleashed his anger on her on an almost daily basis because he had somehow convinced himself that if only my mother weren't around, Josie would return to him. And that just wasn't true. Everything seemed to slowly become calmer. Josie had become the muse for another artist and, I learned later, his lover. I think he whisked her off to England or somewhere. I'm not sure if Papa ever really lost his longing for her, but he seemed to realise it was out of his hands.'

'So what became of you?' I feel heartbroken for this confused child being caught up in a storm of passion and I watch as Agnes begins to twirl one of her stray curls.

'He actually tried to undertake some of the things that my mother used to do. He was so clumsy! I remember him picking me up and sitting me on the table as he tried to fix my favourite red ribbon in my hair. He would bring me to his studio to paint me with my doll dangling at my side. Probably it was one way of keeping an eye on me. I was bounced about for years among extended family members until I got older and was able to fend for myself.'

'Are you still in contact?' Maria seems in awe at how she could have turned all of this around.

'I visited him occasionally in his studio over the years and then noticed he was doing less and less work and was becoming dishevelled and losing weight. I learned from one of his friends that he visited an exhibition at the *Salon* and unwittingly came across a painting called *Red Hair. White Dress*. He didn't seem right after that. So I sought the painting out and with her pale skin and long cascading red hair, I knew that the figure in the painting could only have been my father's tormentor. She didn't mean to be and probably didn't even realise that she was, but men are weak.'

Maria makes an ill-judged attempt to lighten the mood. 'My grandmother used to always say, "If there were no bad women, there would be no bad men."'

Agnes wipes the bread crumbs from the table into the palm of her hand. 'I was not going to watch as this woman destroyed my family twice. So I never visited my father again. I was not my mother.'

* * *

Would my patchouli girl actually stand around this fountain at the Place Pigalle? Would beauty not automatically elevate you to being the navigator of your situation? I have found myself visiting pawn shops over the past few days. What this hopes to achieve, I am not entirely sure, just that if she did fall into the clutches of the Spaniard, then perhaps she too would end up having to pawn her belongings. I dislike being elbowed out of the way by people jostling to cash in on the paltry specimens of their day-to-day lives: odd household utensils, chipped crockery, hats, jewellery, bedraggled clothing, even mattresses.

A fat *marchande de poisons* with blackened front teeth, shoves me aside holding her new umbrella. She would have little use for it, standing behind her stall, but surely she hasn't acquired it in an effort to mimic the fashionable. Does she think that brandishing this umbrella will somehow confer on her the illusion of privilege, of belonging to the bourgeois? It will never work, but she seems smugly convinced of its significance. I look at a rail of coats and think how one piece of attire could be linked to the miserable death of a lost girl.

I have also spread the word of my search among the streetwalkers of Montmartre. I even gave young Joseph a few centimes to keep his eyes and ears open. Then I go to work.

* * *

I don't realise I am being so absentminded until I hear the *patron* shout at me.

'Fleur, you have been carrying around that bowl of soup for five minutes now. Will you serve it to the table by the window there, and if they refuse to pay for it, it's coming out of your wages.'

I carry the soup to the table and place in down while apologising profusely. Walrus jerks his head a little in a beckoning gesture.

'*Mademoiselle*, tell your cook not to be getting so agitated about what is effectively nothing more than flavoured broth. If his ambition is to serve simple food, he can do so without treating his customers as simpletons. What is wrong with the traditional Crécy soup? How complicated can it be to mix carrots, poultry stock and some rice? Even for this kitchen.'

I lower my voice. 'You are just determined to get me into trouble.'

'Nonsense. My mission is to educate the ignorant palate and it is an onerous task I have chosen.'

I swing toward the kitchen with a large silver tray balancing on my palm. The table of men to the left of the door have ordered another round of cognac and they seem to be smoking with more intensity than usual. They are talking about the Spaniard.

'He was last seen in a bistro on Rue La Fayette.'

'That's right, I saw him there myself before heading off home. He was drinking for hours and could barely put one foot in front of the other.'

'A cab driver finishing up for the night saw him lying on the ground, thought he was dead, and got him to his feet. He must have found his own way home.'

'Which of us hasn't tumbled on to the road after a particularly sociable night?'

'Why then are the police so fascinated in talking to all of us? It is damned distracting. I have a huge canvas that I am about to roll up and throw in the Seine because I just can't get it completed. It is nothing short of an assault on my creativity. I don't need any more knocks on my door asking if I've noticed anything suspicious.'

'They seem to be of the opinion all painters could be at risk.'

'At risk of what? Crawling home in a drunken stupor and collapsing when we get there?'

'Collapsing dead, that is the point. It looks as if it was not of his own making, even though many think he deserved it.'

'You see that's the kind of madness that is around, but what have any of us innocuous blackguards ever done to deserve this? Whose wrath could we sensitive creatures of God above have so engaged?'

The others laugh at his feigned despair and dramatic hand wringing. One of the men slaps him on the back.

'Can any of you think of any person that you may have painted an ugly portrait of lately?'

'Well own up, which among you made Madame L'homme and her three children look like a sow with her piglets? I was painting a rather fetching still life at the time, so it wasn't me.'

'Yes, I saw that one, and I mean to say I know her girth is, well, very generous, but for the sake of the woman's vanity, and more importantly, her husband's reputation, could she not have been slimmed down a little?'

'Never, never. Not once in my entire life have I done an ugly portrait of anyone. I have, however, on more than one occasion, painted ugly people.'

The table of men guffaw, a laughter that builds from their chests and is expelled like cannon fire. It is vaguely demented. I serve more cognac. We have a couple of Americans in this evening. Their clothes tell me that they are American. There is a breed of foreigner that come to live in Paris, gentlemen adventurers of a type. Some are society painters, some seem to be respected authors, and some come to trade. The English men speak in low tones of living comfortably on £1,500 a year which sounds to me like an awful lot of money. It must be pleasant to come here and live comfortably. It is probably the most melancholy place to be in the world when you try to live here in poverty.

I watched a young girl sitting on a door step in the pouring rain, trying to shape a hole-size lump of wet newspaper into her soaked boot. I was almost sure that she was crying but it was difficult to distinguish the salty streaming from the wet scene of abject misery. I had a little money. I bent down to put a few coins at her feet. I'm not sure she even registered my offering, with her gloom puddling round the hem of her dress. Lost and destitute girls, like gargoyles in archways and corners, are just part of the overall architecture, their grossness only evident when you care to look closer.

And now I am bending to serve wealthy foreigners a morsel of Paris, a side order of bohemian living, a *digestif* of Gallic conviviality. The patron once put a sign up declaring, 'English Spoken Here' to draw in those passers-by, whose francs would otherwise end up on another's counter. English is only spoken here by irate Englishmen and Americans who feel they are being fleeced and double-charged at every turn by crafty natives. And they are probably right.

The talk of the dead Spaniard continues unabated with theories tossed about like limp lettuce. An unpaid debt that someone lost patience over? A love quarrel? A drunken brawl over a game of cards? The only consensus is the fact that a model found him and then subsequently disappeared. Could it have been her? Did she do more than just find him? When I held open that door for the beautiful girl in the velvet hat, were there secrets in her sweet-tempered face?

We all have secrets and for some reason I always feel as if I have a duty to expose them. Not for the sake of prurience, but for the restorative act of lancing the sickness and purging the system, for secrets are corrosive and the effort to keep them causes enormous strain on body and soul. You can identify the carrier of a secret in the heaviness of a brow, or the flaking of skin, or in unidentifiable rashes that creep over the body, or in the bitten fingernails of even the most tranquil of exteriors. Mine was exposed, of all places, at a séance. I had been to one before and had dismissed them as a charade. At my first séance, we sat around a table holding hands and I knew for a fact that the medium was tapping her foot on a small wooden board that she had slipped in under the table when no one was looking. She was asking the spirits to tap one for 'yes' and two for 'no'. Complete trickery. She even managed to conjure up some smoke. She foretold a life for me of anguished love, which I no doubt could have foretold for myself without the price of an admission ticket.

So when I was invited to go along to another, I think through Henri, I believed that it would be nothing more than an amusing evening, but Madame Xavier was a different beast. Her appearance, clad as she was all in black with a black veil fastened to her hat, did not encourage polite conversation and when she appeared in the room, everyone instinctively cleared a path which she wordlessly cut through, taking her seat at the round dining table. Without being instructed to, everyone sat down and fanned out around the table. I found myself sitting to her right. Madame Xavier pulled the veil from her face and over the top of her hat, and then opened her right palm, indicating to me that I should clasp it. By nodding to the entire group she informed everyone that they were to hold the hands nearest to them.

Madame Xavier looked up toward the ceiling; her head tilted back, her eyelids fluttering. She slowly lowered her chin then closed her eyes. 'Spirit guide, we are here to greet you.'

The assembled group stared at Madame Xavier's face as

her clear voice rang out again, this time a little louder. 'Who do we have here with us?' Her shoulders seemed to take on a squarer appearance and her posture became less upright. 'We are in artistic company.' The voice that came out of the lady in the dark dress now sounded utterly different from her matronly tones. It was harsher and more authoritative. 'Who are you?' Her clear tone returned.

'I am Captain Olivier. The ocean swallowed me up along with my crew and we passed into the spirit world, many moons ago.' The circle around the table almost gasped as one on hearing the Captain's voice, each person transfixed by Madame Xavier's face as her brow took on a heavy sea-worn frown.

'Are you here to help someone?' There was a short pause.

'I have an elderly lady at this side, who wants to apologize for being cruel.' The group looked to each other to see who this could be meant for. Only Henri seemed to have taken it to heart. Madame Xavier's grip on my hand felt stronger and I was afraid to look at her.

'Confusion and prayerful distress has reached me. I have a baby here, but all I can say is that she is being soothed.'

My heart began to pound loudly, colour pumping to my cheeks. I squeezed my eyes tightly closed. No one around that table could have known of my baby, the baby who didn't live for more than a couple of hours. The baby I had as a fifteen-year-old girl in my early days in Paris before I understood that the kindness of men is sometimes contractual and not freely given. My study into how to tell the difference has been an undertaking of many years, and still often, I fail miserably.

'Captain Olivier? Captain Olivier, are you still among us?' Madame Xavier's matronly tones had returned but nothing else came by way of reply. With a trembling breath, Madame Xavier slumped back in her chair, the séance concluded.

My shift here is nearly done. Walrus steadies himself as he rises from his booth and I hand him his hat. His girth speaks of unbridled gluttony but that would be a wrong assumption. His is a nuanced love affair with food. He doesn't gorge on it to satisfy his hunger and then be done, he tries to honour it. And, as if food were something capable of feelings, he hates to reject it, even the blandest lumpiest and most tasteless of specimens placed before him. He must have been a very attentive lover in his youth.

* * *

Distraction from my thoughts of the patchouli girl came with the suggestion by Agnes that we all go to the weekend's masked ball. Maria and I took to the task of transforming ourselves with unseemly gusto as we hunted through several shops, managing to assemble an array of feathers and fake jewels. *Maman* helped us sew them on to elaborate dresses beneath which we wore purple pantaloons. We looked as if we had been tumbled from the Maharaja's trunk, although the image we were aiming for was that of Arabian princesses with peacock feathers pinned to our hair and our kohl-blackened eyes.

Little can match the anticipation of a night of revelry and tonight we are feeling especially flighty. I must have needed this night of diversion more than I had realised. There is a glorious randomness to people who are prepared for nothing but a night of entertainment and possibilities and so we fall in with the indiscriminate swell of eccentricity spilling from one *brasserie* to the next. We weave through jugglers, fire-eaters and tumblers. A man dressed as a woman with a monkey on a leash nods warmly in acknowledgement towards us, the two smiling Arabian princesses, who are, at best, culturally confused in our attire. The street singers fight for their corners with soaring voices their weapon of choice in a duel of supremacy.

Our arrangement is to meet Agnes at the Chat Noir. The tables are small and tightly packed together. There are three musicians playing and singing in the corner between the huge fireplace and the ceiling-high stained-glass window. We nudge our way excitedly through the curtain into the cabaret section of the café and can see Agnes at a busy table chatting and drinking alongside several costumed companions. They are all ignoring the poet who is doing his best to wring out a dismal poem with as much pathos as he can muster while standing on his little platform.

'Ah, my girls. Vermouth all around.'

By the time we have twisted ourselves into the cramped space where two seats have been left for our arrival, the drinks are ready to be raised in a rousing toast.

'To idleness', declared an already tipsy Agnes.

'To idleness', we all enthusiastically concur, my arm bracelets rattling in percussion.

This is the type of setting where I most love to watch Agnes, maybe because I have cast her in the role of a pioneer, exploring the outer boundaries of that mysterious world of aging. I am unfairly expecting her to lay the groundwork, to create the template that I have decided I will use because I have burdened her with my admiration. For example, the impact that she still has on the young men in her company. They fuss over her and hang on to her every word. She is coquettish and flirtatious and the men are jostling each other out of the way to pour her drinks.

I adore my own mother, but her infirmity and feebleness frighten me. To make it more comfortable for me, I try to exaggerate her 'otherness' so that I do not easily find simi-larities between us. I take a twisted pride in the unflattering physical traits that I have inherited from my father, even though my mother's grace would cloak more easily my mis-steps, lack of guile, and plainness. And then I forget my efforts and find myself mirroring her in a regrettably instinctive way. The way we tilt our heads when we are enquiring after someone, the way we tug at the fringes of our hair because we are too aware of our high foreheads despite being told such a forehead speaks of intelligence, the way I feel reas-sured and refined when I splash on my mother's cologne, despite its association with her genteel passivity.

Agnes has braced herself for a pronouncement. She is choosing to introduce the table to us, the recently arrived. 'Ladies, this young man is a fine upcoming artist who is sure to go far. That young man is a sublime poet who would make petticoats quiver with the exquisite tenderness of his words. Beside him, a talented young blade, who, I'm afraid, would not be interested in looking in your direction, my pretties.'

Her strident twinning of 'youth' and 'talent' is frustratingly belittling, almost a slur on everything I hold dear about her. 'Tell me, Agnes, does "youth" always equate to "talent"?'

The young poet, who is masked and cloaked, smiles across the table, evidently deciding to address the question I have posed.

'Yes there is an adoration of youth, or, more correctly, the state of being youthful. We may not be rich in talent, but we are wealthy in vanity and that tends to obscure the real-ity. And when you have someone as discerning as Madame Agnes by your side, then truly you are blessed. With one indulgent glance from her, my self absorption can almost be justified.'

He takes Agnes's gloved hand and kisses the back of it. I roll my eyes; a childish response I know, but I tend only to come up with quick and clever retorts after much deliberation.

'Aren't you the dandy?'

'I would love to be a bohemian, but I couldn't stand the disorder.' He is better at this than I.

'What about the pursuit of individual freedom? Is that the preserve of the young, or only the preserve of the young male?' I feel on firmer ground here. This time the artist responds.

'Surely there is an obligation to pursue individual freedom as a young person, whether male or female.'

'… and your gender shouldn't prohibit you in any way?'

Maria raises her hand. A curious response because usually she in not backward about coming forward. She has been drawing on the table cloth in a distracted manner.

'Who then gets to live with the consequences? You fine gentlemen might end up with no more than an odd or irritating itch, we on the other hand … well, imagine if after even one particularly wild night of pursuing individual freedom, you found yourself growing a whole new person inside you?'

One of the men spurts his drink out. He dabs at his mouth apologetically with a napkin.

'I do beg your pardon. Yes, I can see how that would rather cramp my style. Damned inconvenience I'd have to say.'

The writer laughs and raises his glass. 'To being a man!'

The rest of us, Maria most enthusiastically of all, raise ours in hearty response. 'To being a man!'

Agnes stands up, and everyone else follows suit. 'Now, my lovelies. To the dance! Let's defy nature. Let's go and be deviant.'

We shaped a staggered line and ease towards the gaudy hall, immediately being curled into the throng of dancers. Maria and I take our place on the scuffed wooden floor and stand as each other's *vis-à-vis* for the *quadrille*. One dance blends into the next, waltzes into polkas, one partner into the next, with the sweat on the brow of the conductor glistening under the glow of the lamps. Most people in the feverish crowd are masked. Part of the pleasure of these dance halls is the perfumed anarchy they inspire. These places are looked down on by many in the higher-society ranks because they are the perfect cauldron for lewd and totally uninhibited behaviour. It's well known that while they are condemned in parlour rooms across the city, respectable husbands will just as quickly and fervently sneak off to don a mask and melt into the heady excitement of anonymous love making which is a key promise of the night.

I could be dancing this very instant with an escaped husband. He is short and portly and hidden behind an elaborate eye-piece. Because we are costumed, I think we become kinder and less critical. I am trying to wriggle into a longer hold without outright insulting this person. He is not short enough to be a dwarf, so is simply, therefore, one of life's runts. There is a strange warmth, a breath, on the back of my neck and quickly turning I see it is the writer of our company. He is grinning; his large-brimmed hat cocked low, his mask taking up three-quarters of his face. He executes a quick bow to my portly runt and I am peeled away with a flourish.

'I'm not sure that's entirely allowed.' My tone is of exaggerated primness.

'Should I have begged that sweating man's permission when you know that in truth, this is a rescue mission? I feared you would suffocate, or drown.'

I am pulled assuredly towards him until I am close enough to feel the strands of beads I am wearing indent my skin. This is how you know. A close encounter can be as awkwardly mismatched as wrongly placed jigsaw pieces. Like the first time I sat on a blanket with a boy. It was afternoon, and he had put his arm around me and pulled me close to his side. He then went on to point out the different types of boats and skiffs on the river. I spent the greater part of the afternoon wedged awkwardly against him, staring at a great silver button near his lapel, because I felt too embarrassed to shift my position. To this day, I cannot tell one type of boat from another, but I can recall, even in my sleep, that one great silver button.

This is different. He smells of cedar wood and musk. His hold is strong, like a frame. No – I have an image of a bookcase, and my back the spine of one of its books, and through my flimsy layers his fingers are tracing one verte-bra at a time, inch by inch, as if unsighted and unsure. The width of his palm print is now on the small of my back and I arch towards him. I want him to cover me, in the bestial way that animals in the fields conduct their mating. It is the anonymity of the masks and costumes … it seems to allow for a primitive rendering of lust, an urgency of the immedi-ate, the moment, the now. The costumes are like camouflage, extending permission to indulge in covert behaviour. If I were in my ordinary attire, I know my mind-set would be restrained and disciplined, but here and now, all I am aware of is an overwhelming smell of musk.

And then the conductor swoops his baton with a dramatic flourish and the orchestra takes a break. The masked writer steers me to where Agnes is sitting and pulls out a chair for me. I am composed once more. My fear is that he has always been. That would make me foolish.

'What's your name?' I try to conduct trite civilities. Again the grin and nothing further. He excuses himself and goes off to heartily clap the back of a friend he has just caught sight of and is swallowed up into a small knot of men. I feign diffidence. Agnes fixes her gaze on me.

'I was your age once, Fleur. Time rushes by very quickly. Be steely in your determination to secure yourself a footing in this world. You and Maria must soon find yourself decent positions. Don't fall into the trap of many young women who believe that the only chance for those from low circumstances is to become a grand courtesan. Every young woman born into poverty thinks that they will one day captivate a wealthy man who will drag them out of their position.' Agnes is being kind, but I wasn't born into poverty. I had a good home and a governess. Maria on the other hand is the daughter of a gin-soaked seamstress, and I do not think any less of her for that. Agnes has clearly watched waves of young girls crash against the tide and the waning of the moon. And so she continues, 'Nobody wants to be a brothel dweller for life, or to have to work their fingers to the bone sewing and washing until they're practically blind. But it's a mirage. The beautiful and fêted girl will one day reach thirty, and unless she has amassed enough jewels and possessions by then, well it's back to the brothels and the hovels because she will never be allowed again to mix in respectable company.'

There are ten lives lived in those blue eyes.

'Men are magpies when it comes to stealing beauty. There it is, nice and shiny, and they make off with it until the next glittery thing catches their eye. I'm afraid I'm no longer shiny enough to prove a distraction for too long. Look at you, Fleur. Half a dozen men could pass by this table right now and each would glance. You miss those surreptitious glances when you get to my age. Look, the artists return.'

Both Maria and what I can now assume is a new friend, look slightly flushed, and judging by the peacock feather that drops from Maria's hair to the floor as she takes her seat, it is clear that something more than boisterous dancing has been keeping them occupied.

'I see that my guest list has proved to be a success.' Agnes claps triumphantly.

The writer, on his return to the table, picks up the feather and places it in his inside pocket. The night has reached that point beyond which lay only the dregs. This is something that experience teaches you, so Agnes rises and immediately everyone else prepares to leave without any real decision being voiced. The third young male companion, the blade as she referred to him, who has said very little throughout the entire evening, seems content to allow Agnes to hook his arm. It is almost as if this was his only purpose.

She kisses Maria and me on the cheek and announces that she is taking her troupe home with her. 'I need a ring of safety until I reach my front door. You girls will understand.'

I'm a little disappointed that there is no protestation on any of the young men's parts. But Agnes had decreed that she needs their companionship the whole way home, and nobody was going to object. Maria and I link arms and heave each other up the cobbled streets towards home. Throngs of people are milling about, their shadows partnering up under the lights of the Boule Noir and the L'Élysée dance halls. We are in that lovely part of the night where bellies are full and heads are light and people fall reluctantly and unthinkingly into their homeward strides until only echoes remain like lingering, watchful ghosts.

✳ ✳ ✳

'It's only me, *Maman*.' I whisper softly so as not to startle her. She often falls asleep on the chair when I am out for a long time. She worries and I think feels lonely. I fold her shawl into a triangle shape. She is like a bird, bony and fragile. Her thin neck seems too weak to support her head; her buttoned boots seem abnormally large attached to her twigs of ankles. I am always afraid that she will topple over or take flight on an unexpected gust of wind. My role is like that of scaffolding, something she can hold on to, brace herself against and feel supported by. I shoe-shuffle her towards the bed we share. It is late, so I just unbutton her boots and pull the blankets up – three of them because they are each tattered in their own way. A prayer is mouthed towards the ceiling in the belief, no doubt, that you can speed them heavenward if the trajectory is correct.

I need to do some clearing up. My propensity to ignore clutter has led to some rather unpalatable discoveries such as mouldy bread, and once a mouse living in the fabric of a chair. I evicted it and vowed to reform my habits, or at least modify them, so I try to make the effort before falling into bed.

There is a small plate of cured sausage and some left-over bread which I'll cover with a cloth. Both can be used perhaps, for breakfast. I clear some papers from the fireside chair in case she sits on them and I also move the hat to a safer place. A hat? This is not mine. My mother has not owned such a confection in a very long time. It is soft to the touch like the fur of a kitten. Is it velvet? The rim is wide and floppy, the ribbon: green satin; the decoration: a little bird. I crush it towards my face … and smell patchouli.

AIRY FLORAL

Hiding in plain sight. It's the trick of scoundrels and renegades and I know I am neither, but who will believe me? I can picture the scene from an observer's point of view. There is a gaggle of about a dozen young ladies strolling around the various stalls of the *fête*, gossiping and munching on toffee apples and waffles. An older woman is chaperoning them as they pause by the bandstand to listen to the booming brass sounds. There is one girl looking out of place. She is hanging back a little and isn't paired with any of them in particular. She is clutching a large Japanese-print bag with bamboo handles, and not the frilly parasols of everyone else in the group. And while the others all wear splendid bonnets decorated with flowers and fruits, this one young lady is bareheaded. And that would be me. I am unsure where I left my hat in these mad few days since I flung myself down those stairs in an undignified escape attempt. He wouldn't stop mauling me and I had only come to be painted. I probably should have slapped him the first time he tried, but I was concerned I may have been overreacting in the company of a sophisticated artist. I cannot explain the rage that bubbled inside of me though. It shocked me. I did everything in my power to supress it and to present myself only as a scented scabbard from which he could draw his genius. I know now I should not have drunk wine with him as that must have seemed like an invitation, or at least approval of time spent in his company. The wine, the fumes, my newness to Paris – how did I so easily allow all of that to blunt my judgement, my common sense, my perception? How did I so easily and willingly forget my past? To forget those other hands that mauled me? Is there something about me? How am I still so foolish, so stupid, so naïve?

The confusing thing is that I felt perfectly safe when I was completely disrobed and arranged on his couch. I did not sense a single flicker of lust as he divided his attention between me and his large canvas. It was not until I began to dress that somehow there ceased to be any censorship in his behaviour and that last time, when I was layering my clothes on behind the screen and he creaked one panel ajar to step around to where I was, I knew. He was unbuttoning himself even as he steered me by the back of my neck towards the couch and as I lay face down with my camisole and petticoat pushed far up my back I tried to focus on the cravat that I was somehow holding in my hand. It had been hanging on a hook behind the screen and I must have lifted it off just as he reached around for me. It wasn't mine. It was, however, oddly comforting pressed against my nose and wafting of summer gardens. I closed my eyes to block out the brutish rhythm, and became lost in soft pale rose petals and geraniums and lavender. With a final withered grunt, he rolled away. I slid off the couch and slowly made my way back behind the screen, then finished dressing with a newfound urgency before finally dashing hurriedly down the stairs. And then things become a bit disjointed. I recall bumping into a *gendarme*. I was tear stained and dishevelled and insisted he take down my details as I had just been the victim of a brutal attack, but there must have been something disbelieving in his eyes as I did not get the sense that he was prepared to do anything about it.

I'm still viewing the sequence of events at the *fête* as an outsider to try to piece it all together. After several musical renditions, the chaperone claps her hands, telling the girls to fall in line, that it was time to head back to the school. The young ladies, many of them hooking arms, sway back towards the railway station in giggles and gossip. The bareheaded girl sticks close by them. They secure a carriage and after a few minutes, the train groans off. The girl with the cherries on her hat nudges her friend.

'There's that strange creature again. See her with the odd bag.' Both girls strain to take in a side view.

'She doesn't look very well. She seems to be nodding off and look there's sweat on her forehead.'

'Madame Gouloumes!' Both girls scream as they watch the stranger tumble forward to the ground.

Which is why when I opened my eyes, I was aware of a cool cloth on my forehead with a pink-cheeked lady stroking my cheek and telling me I had given them such a fright. Standing rigidly behind her is a heavy-bosomed woman with a stern face.

'Now let me get you some tea.' The pink-cheeked lady seems to be cooing, not actually speaking. I finger the lace scalloped edging on the crisp white sheet which is tucked tightly, entombing me in this softly corpulent mattress. Everything about this room is fresh and airy, from the soft blue stripes of the wallpaper, to the white floor boards, to the delicate curtains daintily pirouetting in and out of the open window frame. But that conversation is seeping like a grey pall over this shimmering haven. The conversation I over-heard while sitting on the omnibus. At first it was nothing but random words, punctuating my trailing thoughts. But then they became more fluidly insistent and focused. The two men were discussing the gruesome story of a painter who was found dead. I listened just long enough to sud-denly realise that I knew who they were talking about and I had a rising sense of dread. I gathered up my few belong-ings and wandered aimlessly before falling in with a group of girls on an outing. And now here I am, in a strange bed, wearing somebody's nightgown. The lady with the stern face has not moved.

'Your skirts and underskirts were all stained, with mud or paint or something.'

The soft-cheeked lady nods in agreement. 'Yes, and you were burning up.'

'We weren't sure how long it was going to take you to come around, so I sent for the police. I thought they could help. Is there someone we can get in touch with for you, now that you are awake?'

I elbow myself up into a sitting position against the bal-last of soft pillows surrounding me. 'Honestly, I'm fine now. Where am I?'

'You have found your way into Madame Gouloumes' Boarding School for Young Ladies. But lie back and rest; you are not ready to get up yet.'

I would love to lie back and rest, but that could be my

undoing. I have to be forcefully matter-of-fact. 'Really. My mother will be waiting for me. She will be so cross. We are going on a trip, and I was meant to meet up with her, only I got distracted by the *fête*.'

'But how did you get into such a weakened state?' Of course they are going to want to unravel the mystery of the strange girl who collapsed among them, so I must find my clothes. The look of disbelief that I saw in the *gendarmes*' eyes makes me want to just go back home, home to the Loire Valley, without any further explanations to anyone about any of this ill-conceived adventure here.

'I was being careless and had a bit of a tumble in the park, and I also forgot to eat. I thank you so much for your kindness, but my mother will be worried by now.'

'Very well then, if you really feel you are up to it.'

My clothes are brought over to the bed and laid out piece by piece, as if dressing a cloth mannequin. On hearing the door pulled and clicked shut, I anxiously begin layering my clothes on, knowing that my haste will not be misconstrued, as they all believed my mother to be waiting somewhere for me. The banister is highly polished and my free hand skates in one long sweep until it is stopped at its end, by a large carved acorn. I can hear the voices of a man and a woman coming from a small front room. Clutching my bag in front of me – there it is a mere few steps away – I see the front door. I am nearly there, but I first have to pass the room with the voices.

'Ah, Babette.' Madame Gouloumes is calling me from just inside the open door. Glancing in, I can see a neatly set table with a dainty cake-stand, cups and saucers and patterned plates with Madame earnestly pouring tea from a small silver pot. The policeman nods his appreciation.

'The Inspector here wants to speak with you.' With that, Madame rises as if taking flight from a nest, a gracefully upward soaring and she leaves the room, closing the door behind her. This room is different. It is more of an upholsterer's paradise, in complete contrast to the clean lines of the bedroom. I feel sure that the young ladies are normally not allowed in here because there is something louche about the way the chairs and sofas are over stuffed and their backs overly swayed. They seem to be an invitation to relax one's elegant posture and instead to lounge and sprawl gracelessly. How else to arrange yourself on such designs? You would have to almost fight against their shape for the more fitting attitude would be to simply slouch. Except of course for the chairs at the table where the policeman is still sitting and which Madame has vacated.

'Mademoiselle Fournière, I'm glad I've caught up with you.' The inspector's words are muffled as he wipes his mouth with a large starched serviette.

'Sir?'

'Have a seat, please.'

I quietly obey and rest my bag on the floor beside my chair.

'You see there are just a few questions that I feel you may be able to help me with. Maybe coincidences, always possible.' He is smiling, but it is not a reassuring gesture. His arms are now crossed and he is staring at me, unblinkingly – which makes me double my own nervous blinking in an effort to compensate.

'You are familiar with a painter called Manuel. Is that correct?'

'Monsieur … ? Let me think.'

'No, Mademoiselle, you may be misunderstanding me, but this is not a parlour game. A young laundry girl was able to tell me that you were probably the last person to see him alive.'

I am genuinely confused. 'I'm sorry sir. I don't think I know such a laundry girl.'

'She said you stumbled out of this painter's apartment in a distressed state late on Thursday evening, and she came to your aid.'

Of course. There was the slightly inebriated young girl who had come to see why I was upset and crying. I must have told this young stranger how I had just been attacked. I do remember her trying to comfort me, because to my shame, even in those moments, I was aware there was a mouldy smell rising in vapours from her dress when she went to give me a brief embrace. In a disjointed tumble, she asked me my name, the painter's name, how much I was being paid for the sitting and whether I had any intention of going back.

'Now when I think of it, yes, I do recall coming across a young girl.' Was it before or after that, when I unloaded my misery to the implacable *gendarme*?

'So the next morning, that very same painter who you admitted had callously assaulted you, is found dead. Then today, I get a message from this fine establishment for ladies that they are in care of a waif who could only mumble her name before passing out. And look at you now, all poised as if to leave. Are you going somewhere?'

'I can assure you, that painter was very much alive when I ran out of his studio.'

'Yes, well, mademoiselle, if our work could rely on assurances alone, our jobs would be so much simpler. I'm sure it wouldn't surprise you to hear that thieves often assure me they haven't robbed and murderers that they haven't killed.'

He stands, in a much more laboured way than Madame and not in an unkindly way, takes my elbow directing me too to stand. 'There are just a few things that need to be cleared up. You'll appreciate that.'

Hugging my bag, I am steered out of the room and towards the front door. Many of the girls who were at the *fête* are standing like primly arranged ornaments on the buffed stairs, with the pink-cheeked lady and Madame Gouloumes like two mismatched bookends standing at the bottom. I can just about hear one of the girls whispering behind her hand to her friend on the step in front of her, 'We could all have been murdered.'

* * *

If that observer in the park could describe me now, she would see someone in a state of absolute shock and terror. She would have watched as I stood in the dock, pleading my innocence while I was being referred to repeatedly as a 'wretched creature'. She would have listened as someone, I'm not sure who, spoke on my behalf using terms like 'delicate damsel' and an 'inherent piety' and she would have witnessed a gruff, whiskered *gendarme* calibrate my distress with somehow being directly responsible for it and she would have heard it concluded that I was indeed, some kind of deviant from which the world needed to be made safe. All this has been recorded for I watched intrigued, as reporters condensed the proceedings and my upset for the leisurely fireside reading of others.

All I can see here through this high grilled window are two cell-cars clattering out of the cobbled courtyard on their way to the Justice Palace with more prisoners. It looks almost elegant. One of the covered cars being drawn by two black horses, and the other by two white horses. The two drivers up front have blankets across their knees and if I make my eyes squint I can imagine that these women are being taken to a ball.

* * *

This place is a noisy clanking hell. From the very first day that I passed through the arched front entrance, it has been as if I was clamped in armour of fear, rigid and cold against my skin. With that first tentative walk down that long corridor, an ocean of noise swept over me. The corridor seemed to narrow as I got closer to the dormitory where I would be staying. My first glimpse of the room was of a dimly lit space with a dozen or more beds looming like shadowy humped-back beasts. Wherever there was a hint of brightness, it was caged in grilled mesh. My eyes are slowly adjusting, but my bed is not the sanctuary that I crave from the chaos. I used to love that sensation of sinking deep under the covers when the night turned inky, but here I lay down my fearful throbbing head and pray for dawn. My fingernails tear at my skin each night as the bedbugs and lice gorge on my compliance.

If I was one of those reporters in the court, I would make a note of each class of humanity thrown here together, from the streetwalkers to the petty thieves to the murderers. I would easily describe them all as 'wretched creatures' and I so completely out of place. Several of these women have killed their husbands or lovers in what are dismissed as 'passionate accidents'. 'Passionate accidents?' I would make a note of that. I feel no safer here in my sheath of womanhood than I did with that brute of a painter. Each night, on this pathetically thin mattress, I try to close my mind to the night-time activities of the other women around me. Though I attempt to make myself as small as possible, more than once I have felt a hand reach in under my covers and snake across my breasts. My first instinct was to scream, but it only seemed to cause amusement. I did not know that other women would do such a thing. My pleading to be moved to another cell was greeted by the nuns as if they were deaf and me an unstable mute.

The brief walk across the cobbled courtyard to the chapel blows fresh air on to my face. It is the softest of reminders that there is something else out there, an otherness, and a power generating a life that can not be confined by the sheer height of these walls, that there is still a God. Every single part of me feels as if it has been breached and a briefly soothing puff of air on my face is like a mother's kiss. Yes, you can still hear bird song, but to my ears it is like a taunt.

It is clear that the nuns deliberately pay no attention to the sordidness of the darkened dormitories. On the other hand, they do dislike people being loud or disruptive and intervene immediately. I have resorted to screaming *'La Marseillaise'* at the top of my lungs each night until they move me to a cell which holds older prisoners. Any ensuing punishment for my bad behaviour would be worth it to be able to ease into even one night of peaceful rest. But I need more time to get my bearings and to work out the rhythms of prison life.

The workshop is not much more pleasant. All the women sit in rows on wooden slat-back chairs facing the same direction, while a nun perches on a high stool at a desk, supervising the mending work. It isn't a very big room and even though there are a few ceiling lamps, they do not throw light very effectively so we all sit here like ill-defined spectres. The stove has a reassuring solidity. I have given myself a few pin pricks because there is an elderly woman rocking back and forth in the front row, and I keep glancing at her.

She is like a disturbed metronome, her straggly grey hair the texture of fraying wool.

'Don't stare at her.'

Cécilia is the nearest thing I have to a friend here. I was initially very wary of the coarse young girl with her calloused hands and scarred chin. I am still not convinced that on my first day in the workshop, when I went to sit down and ended up crashing to the floor, that it was, as she claimed, an accident and that she hadn't deliberately pulled my chair too far back for me to sit on. But when the nun slipped down from her stool and, pushing chairs aside, brandished a long stick over Cécilia as if to strike. I apologised profusely, blaming my own carelessness. I knew from Cécilia's wry smile that we would probably be friends. The young prostitute who was also a thief, had been in and out of this prison three times now, and her unperturbed attitude is vaguely comforting. I am still in awe and my naiveté is fodder for the amusement of the unscrupulous.

'See that bonnet she is wearing; you'll see some of the women with the same bonnet. It is a sign that they have syphilis. She has gone a bit mad. She is meant to be confined to silence, which is also driving her crazy – not that she needs much help.'

'What is she in here for?'

'Who knows at this stage, probably arsenic in her husband's chocolate drops or something?' We try to muffle our giggles with our sewing. 'A lot of these crones could just as easily chop the pricks off their men for messing with other women, but arsenic is easier and cleaner. There are some very good poisoners in here.'

'Not so good if they're in here.' When did my humour get so black?

'Tell me Babette; are you sorry you ever came to Paris?' Cécilia is giving me a friendly nudge. I lower my head to better conceal my whispering.

'You could say that. Do you know: I miss the smell of lavender. I thought for a second when I stood at an open window this morning that I could smell lavender. I closed my eyes and took a long, deep breath, but nothing.'

'Floor polish probably.'

'Our housekeeper wore some kind of lavender perfume around the house and she would give me these crushing hugs, and I could smell lavender off my own skin even after she left.'

'So you had servants and a housekeeper, and she wore lavender perfume and gave you lots of hugs and one day you woke up and thought: life is too easy, I think I'll go to Paris! You didn't want the famous Saint Lazare Prison to be one of life's mysteries?'

I came to Paris to have an adventure, in part to escape. How feeble sounding is that? How stupid? I can't even remember what calculated construct I gave to my mother by way of justification and reassurance. It wasn't duplicitous, just outrageously optimistic. I began to miss home almost the minute I stepped off the train. I had wanted to re-invent myself, to be more strident and daring. It's why I began to wear patchouli. Patchouli was free-spirited knee tremblers in back alleys. It was absinthe that burnt your throat on the way down and made you bang your glass on the table and let out a loud whoop. It was desire and recklessness. Patchouli was Paris. Lavender hinted at warm bread and plump maternal women. It spoke of well-behaved young ladies who blushed easily. It gave a nod to chaste couples stealing kisses under apple trees. It was a pleasant hug from a housekeeper.

But I can feel the tiny hairs on my forearms bristling even now, when I think of how it transported me as that foul painter violated me. That sweet-smelling cravat that I was able to bury my nose in and think of butterflies, as if summer had brushed my lips. It had to be hers, because she moved in a floral symphony, her eyes so vivid they made me think of lily ponds. She looked soft and rounded and kind. The young laundry was able to point me to her home. I have no friends here yet. The girl remembered being given money by her. 'I'm not ashamed to beg', she kept saying … and I didn't care. I just wanted to know where the bright-eyed girl lived. The girl thought she lived with her mother. Fleur. How appropriate a name.

I pushed the door open when no one answered my knock. It was an impoverished home with little welcoming about it. I could see a small pile of linen with a sewing box resting on top of it. There on the table was a plate with some strong, almost rancid-smelling meat partially covered by a plate and some bread that was slightly mouldy. A shawl was draped over the back of one of the fireside chairs and two plump red cushions, the only thing of colour in the entire room, popped out from the jaded tapestry of the couch. I was afraid to loiter. I quietly stole out of the room again. Now that I think of it, that must be where I left my hat.

The old woman at the front here is getting more agitated. She is rubbing her arms and legs vigorously and under these dim lights; it's as if she is rubbing them raw. I am unable to continue sewing. Cécilia is leaning into me.

'She thinks she has leprosy. This used to be a hospital for lepers, oh two hundred years ago. She's convinced she caught it from something here.'

The woman is now standing up and swaying. The sister is angrily climbing down from her stool. It's a comical manoeuvre as she is short legged, so there is an unseemly pivot of the hips before she can manage to plant both feet on the ground. She is trying to settle the old woman with a stern tone and the air is bristling with anticipation. And there it is, in the flash of a second, the old woman lunging forward and placing her two hands, palms down, on the stove. She screams in agony and the smell of singed flesh clings to the air like gauze.

She is hauled away, screaming and dragging her legs.

'I don't want to be shot. I don't want to be shot.'

I feel suddenly convulsed in shivers as if my heart will jump out of my chest and I am winded of breath. I feel Cécilia's arm around my shoulder.

'Hey there. She is only a mad bat.'

'I didn't do it, Cécilia. I shouldn't be here.' My words sputter between snatched breaths. She just nods.

'None of us should. We're survivors, struggling in the only way we know how, and they punish us for it. They should give us a medal.'

* * *

My name is being called – a strange, hollow echo reverberating off the bars. I can feel its vibrations as I press my cheek to the closed hatch.

'Babette Fournière. Would Babette Fournière make herself known?'

The key is unlocking our door even as this request is being hollered, so they know I'm here. I stand to attention. I am learning to respond to commands with the compliance of a beaten puppy.

'You're leaving here, gather your things.'

I'm leaving? Of course I'm leaving. Somebody has realised their terrible mistake. I swiftly gather my small bundle of things. I am standing in the plain grey prison dress with the striped apron that everyone is assigned on arrival. My blood is pumping as I follow the guard down the long corridor. I allow myself a small smile. I'll have to write a note for Cécilia to say my goodbyes. Why has the guard stopped so abruptly? I nearly bump into him. He growls and with two large keys unlocks the door and pulls it ajar. Something has gone wrong. I am standing at the other side of the door, numbly aware that it is being locked again leaving me on the wrong side of it. I can feel a pathetic whelp rise through my tightened throat. There is a gap in the door and I must be heard.

'Wait, you've made a mistake. I'm Babette Fournière. I should be getting out.'

Someone is laughing. Laughing? Swinging around I see two young girls, one only slightly younger looking than me. The younger of the two is imitating me.

'I should be getting out', she mimics. I can hear myself scream, an involuntary convulsion that would under any other circumstances have embarrassed me hugely, and one by one I throw each item that I have been clutching at the young mimic who is swinging this way and that to avoid being hit. From somewhere near me, the older girl walks over and picks up my pieces of clothing while chastising the young girl for being nasty. I slump on to a bench, the only furniture in the cell.

'Here, you'd want to be very careful about hanging onto your outside clothes because one day you will need them. Many a girl has nothing to wear when it's time to leave. They could be stolen from you at any time, so I wouldn't go flinging them about if I was you.'

I suddenly am aware of how grimy I am. I feel as if I have been dipped in something. My face must resemble – I don't know – probably these ugly children swarming around me.

'Why was I moved here? I thought I was leaving.' The older girl is the only one I feel has the wit to respond sensibly.

'What age are you?'

'I'm sixteen. Nearly seventeen.'

'Better to say you're fifteen, nearly sixteen. You probably should have been brought here first. This is a children's cell. Well for younger inmates anyway. I'm Paulette.'

I am a little embarrassed at first to take her outstretched hand because I feel so dirty, but then Paulette is even filthier, though she does have a pleasant face. She gestures to a corner of the room where I can roll out a mattress and without saying another word, I nestle as best I can and try to fall asleep. There is no stillness in this place. It is as if we are trapped in the belly of a beast. We have been swallowed whole and everything is just rumbling around us. We are swirling innards and I feel as if I can't breathe.

* * *

I must somehow have slept because this morning is sharp and clear and I was able to find Cécilia so we could walk around the courtyard.

'Babette, you must not let this place get you down. Look, you are too pale already. Keep your shoulders back. There is a Saint-Lazare walk that I would recognise from two streets away. It's a broken walk, as if holding up your head was too much of an effort.' I feel her thumb and forefinger prise up my chin. 'I'm warning you now, the minute you start thinking like a prisoner, you begin to look like one.'

'What am I going to do, Cécilia? My mother would be too ashamed to come and visit me. I told her how well I was doing in Paris and not to worry about me so I can't turn around now to tell her where I am. She would disown me.'

* * *

'I will keep in touch with you. You see, I'm getting out in a few days time. I'll send you parcels.'

I am shocked to find myself starting to cry at this sudden news. I'm of course happy for Cécilia – but – not really. She looks as if she belongs here, as if this were an extension of her sordid life that she will resume as soon as she snatches that first breath of freedom. I need to sit down. Cécilia is scowling at me.

'Now listen to me. Don't be pathetic. Do you think I'd still be alive if I did nothing but sit on a bench and cry?'

I try to extinguish my sniffling with the cuff of my sleeve. Another bastion of respectability gone, in one mucous snot trail.

'Oh, forget it. I've enough to worry about. You have only yourself to rely on once you get out there. The quicker you learn that the better.'

She stands up and starts to walk away. I am inexplicably bereft. She is halfway across the courtyard when she stops and walks back towards the bench again. Standing with her hands on her hips, she shakes her head. Taking her seat again, she starts laughing.

'Look at you, a pretty girl with nice manners and big words. Do you know what I would do if I were you? I'd find the grandest house, run by the smartest Madame and I'd live in luxury. You get lots of lovely clothes and a nice place to live. A cousin of mine lives like that. Her side got the good looks. My side was fish gutters from way back.' She turns my hand over and strokes my palm. 'See the difference? Your lovely long fingers and my short stubby ones? There would never be room for the likes of me in Madame's house.'

'I've no idea how long I'm going to be here for.'

'They can keep you as a subordinate, seeing as you've nowhere to live and you're only sixteen. They could keep you until you're twenty-one, unless someone claims you. You haven't been charged yet. If they find you guilty, that's another story.'

Cécilia tilts her head and takes in my despair with what is clearly pure pity, and this almost makes me feel worse.

'Can I not contact your mother?'

'No. She would die of shame.'

'Is there anyone in Paris then?'

I pretended to my mother that I had secured a position as a companion to an elderly lady and had sent her a letter filling her with the delights of my new arrangement. I had intended to carry out this ruse for only a month or two but damned unfortunate circumstances overtook everything. I know no one in Paris, except that girl. I have kept her cravat tucked in among my belongings. What am I thinking? What succour could I possibly expect when I remember her pathetic little lodgings? She wouldn't have a clue who I was anyway.

'No, Cécilia, I can't think of anyone who would know or care about me.'

We find ourselves walking several laps around the court-yard in a soothing, numbing perambulation, until everyone is summoned inside.

* * *

Staring expectantly at the door of the workshop, waiting for Cécilia to come bursting through, I realised: Cécilia is gone.

Each stitch now is a stabbing reminder of my loneliness, each finished hem another yard of passing time. My cellmate, Paulette, tried to cheer me up by reminding me that Cécilia was a habitual offender and would probably be back. I have mixed feelings about this. I hope for Cécilia's sake that this wouldn't turn out to be the case and know it was selfish to wish otherwise, though it didn't stop me looking longingly at each new intake of women hoping to recognise her face. True to her word, Cécilia sent a parcel with soap and a comb and some ribbon within a week of her departure. She also included a note with her cousin's address. Sweet of her, as I know in her world to live at the Madame's house like her cousin would be the height of aspiration, but when I get out of here, I am going home.

I'm wondering what it will be like to leave here. Like an animal adjusting to its environment, I sometimes find my step lighter, my mood even a little jocular. I squabble with my cell mates as if they were my little sisters and not the urchins that I would normally step cautiously around if I encountered them on a street. Sometimes even these bars don't seem to obstruct my view, and could as easily be curtain panels to be simply parted with one sweep of my hand. The wagons are arriving with another batch of women. Staring at them, you can see the first timers, the way their heads jerk about to take in their surroundings. You can see the disbelief in their faces. Then there are those whose step is arrogant, assured in its defiance, a step of anticipation where they will again meet up with old friends.

'Babette'. Paulette touches my arm. What is normally a gesture of kindness, in a place like this, usually heralds some bad news. 'Have you heard?'

I search her eyes, pale insipid pools. Eyes that ceased to be excited about anything a long time ago, despite her very young years.

'Cécilia is dead. She was stealing in someone else's patch. You don't do that. There are rules about them things. Her body was dumped in an alley and her face was smashed in.'

I inhale deeply and nod primly.

'Thank you for telling me.' I walk down the corridor away from her and feel my legs buckle and blackness descending.

* * *

The sound of a nun rapping her ring on the bars of their door has disturbed me.

'Disinfection. Disinfection, girls.'

I pull myself up on to one of my elbows and rub my eyes. 'What is she on about, Paulette?'

Paulette just groans and pulls her blanket over her face. 'Not again. They may as well give up the battle against lice, because the lice are winning. *Merde.*'

The youngest girl in the cell jumps up and began to dress. 'The quicker we get out there, the sooner it's over. Trust me Babette; you don't want to be standing around waiting for this.'

I am immune to whatever new misery they choose to bestow on me so throw off my blanket. I have ceased caring about trying to fix my hair, and am no longer concerned about the dirt streaking my face. Everyone lines up with their backs against the wall, so that when the nun doubles back, we are all ready to be marched out. Trudging through several corridors, we eventually fall in behind girls and women of all shapes, sizes and ages, all of whom had shuffled to a stop outside a wash block, where the laundry is normally done.

I can hear the large wooden door being creaked open at regular intervals, while a head count is shouted out, 'Next four. One, two, three, four. Stop.' And it is slammed shut again. Soon I am second in line in front of the closed door, and my hands begin to involuntarily clench, but going through that door is the only option.

'Next four. One, two, three, four. Stop'

As the door is closed behind me, I see I am standing in a white cold room with stone floors. There are several tubs on the ground and two hefty flush-faced nuns with their sleeves pushed up passed their elbows, standing among them.

'Clothes off. Hang them on that rail. And on your way out, take some of that straw with you for your monthly flow.'

The other three girls are immediately doing as instructed without any fuss, and in my brow-beaten timidity, I simply copy their actions. A nun standing by one of the tubs gestures for me to go over to her. She has a brush clenched in one of her hands and stands with her knuckles on her hips or thereabouts as she is just one squat column of fat without any curves to indicate that she is not a big pasty sausage with an apron on. Again, the other girls, without even a whimper of indignation, walk straight over to the tubs as if they have no awareness of their nakedness. My skin has pimpled with the cold and my instinct is to try and cover myself with my hands and arms. The nun grabs hold of one of my wrists and then the other, shaping me into a crucifixion position.

'Oh for heaven's sake, stupid girl. There is no room for modesty here.' She plunges the brush into the tub and begins scraping on my arms and shoulders and breasts and stomach. The water is very cold and is mixed with something that smells like chlorine. She kicks my legs further apart and drags the brush over the inside of my thighs, then spins me around while she works on my shoulders, down my back and over my buttocks. I fix my gaze on one tiny squashed fly on the wall in front of me and it calms my breathing from a panicked flutter to a steady piston of strength. With each inhale, I curse this hell hole and everyone in it. With each exhale, I swear that I will reclaim every single raw inch of my skin and will, one day, have it caressed only in silk. I think of lavender. I think of patchouli.

MUSKY OAK-MOSS

The night of the masked ball has been like a sweetly lingering shower of summer rain on overheated skin. The dance
itself a rolling tide of every species of attire and then that hot
breath on my neck and the tentative crush of a man fleetingly
against me. It is difficult to frame these moments in isolation
when my inclination is immediately to audition each male as
a potential suitor. I have banished many poor unsuspecting
men from being the future father of my children without
even their vaguest awareness of my existence. It is, I suppose,
easy to do this in the café where men are in the privacy of a
convivial meal among their friends. Standards are relaxed and
true natures are revealed. I go along, merrily crossing them
off my list for crimes against my own contrived notions of
what is acceptable: foul language used too frequently – 'X';
being more disrespectful about women than your average
male – 'X'; surreptitious touching of another male dining
companion using the cover of sociability – 'X, and very con-

fused!' Sometimes there are subtle things that edge them out, like a certain timidity that would take too much work and effort to help them overcome. Sometimes it is much more significant, like the game playing that an otherwise covetable man starts to engage in when it comes to settling the account at the end of a night. You see them, the ones that fumble in their pockets for those few seconds too long while all around him are gathering up their contributions. In some, it is developed to such an art that only I notice that the game-player has not actually parted with any coins.

And sometimes, I find myself studying a customer and wondering, just wondering. However, the more I feel drawn to a man, the further I will backtrack. There is nothing more deadly than unrequited love and I am unsure if it is more dangerous to be at the receiving end of it or to be in the thralls of it. I ponder this because of something I read in this morning's *Le Matin*. A few columns to the left of the sport, was the sad tale of a young Alsacienne, a pretty brunette called Marie Herbert. As she entered her room, with her key still in her hand, she was met by a Monsieur Million who worked as the *valet de chambre* of the house. He was in love with Marie but she didn't want to marry him. He became angry so she turned to leave the room again, but he stood in front of her and then took out a revolver that he had been carrying on his person. With two shots, she lay dead. He had been in the service of M. Dorneth since July 1881 while Marie had only worked there from May of last year. Million confessed all of this to the *Commis de crime*. Her body has been transported to the morgue.

Now she is dead. He, however, is left to live with the misery of what he has done to a woman he loved. It must be like a hundred thousand cuts that he will eventually bleed to death from. You see for a mere five centimes, a newspaper column can teach you a valuable life lesson. I folded away *Le Matin* and have been quite unable to get Million and Marie Herbert out of my head all day. I need to re-focus my attentions to pleasant and unchallenging men who are not capable of great passion. I think that would make for a much easier life.

* * *

As I approach, I see Maria sitting by the fountain, eating ice cream with her face tilted to the sun.

'Maria, do you remember telling me once that you could probably survive on ice cream alone?'

'That's because it was such a rare treat. My mother would sometimes forget to feed me, so ice cream seemed something I could get for myself. But of course, we could hardly ever afford it.'

Maria was always the more street wise of the two of us, scampering about all wild and uncultivated. There was something wilful and rampant about her which was evident from the first time I came across the tiny girl selling vegetables from a stall. It was shortly after I began working at the café that we discovered we lived in the same area of Montmartre and we vowed with the earnestness of new best friends, that we would never live anywhere else. It was theatre, it was cabaret. The night sky draped like a velvet cloak over the nooks and darkened crannies, tucking us into its folds.

'Fleur, I have some news for you. I was back at the ladies painting group, you know, I've been there a couple times before, and I overheard a young mademoiselle regaling with great drama how a murderess was trapped at her boarding school.'

'Intriguing.'

'This girl is a new student – bit of an attention seeker – so I was only partly paying attention, but she said this person was arrested in broad daylight for the murder of a painter and was taken away by a police inspector. Well, when I heard there was a painter involved, I deliberately fell into conversation with her at the end of the class. Honestly, you'd swear I hadn't been sitting there in the nude for the previous three hours, the look she gave me, as if, who did I think I was, suddenly trying to talk to her. It's all right for me to be sprawled out all legs akimbo, but to dare to try to strike up a conversation with her?'

'Maria, will you get to the point!'

'Of course. Anyway, I wanted to get some information on who the painter was but she had no idea. However, the murderess, as she kept calling her, was a young girl called Babette. She described her as being very beautiful with lovely bright eyes, not ones that you would expect a murderess to have. Then she went on to have a conversation with herself about whether the girl's eyes were lovely or evil.'

'Babette. She could be a Babette. Is it her?'

'This girl was not from Paris and she had been modelling for a painter who she thinks was Spanish, and all she could tell me was that the girl was taken away by the an inspector.'

My heart is racing and there's a pulsing at my temples. I know that it is her. I feel it as vividly as if we were two dabs of colour on the Spaniard's palette and with a casual swipe of his brush, we have bled into one intense swirl.

'Thanks, Maria. I'm late and have to get to work. We'll talk soon.'

She is shouting after me. 'Fleur, that was well over a month ago, at least. I kept missing you.'

It's strange when your mind suddenly becomes flooded with information that requires teasing out. Maybe it's just me, but the more logic I have to employ, the more easily distracted my thoughts become. I see there is a cash sale on at reduced prices. Big bold letters are screaming at me from the large shop window, 'New & Fashionable Stock, previous to Stock Taking'; 'Sale of Special Purchase Ladies Dress Materials, Prints, All-Wool Flannels, and Gloves, about 1,000 Pairs of all kinds'; 'Cotton and Merino Stockings, not in any case more than Half-Price', '700 Men's, Boys' and Youths' Ready-Made Tweed & Black Worsted Suits'.

See now that is a good sale. What must a thousand pairs of gloves look like? How high would that stack? And here in the window of the pharmacy, my goodness there is a cure for everything, 'Hair Destroyer: Special Depilatory removes hair from the face, neck and arms, sent by post, secretly packed for 54 stamps'; 'Hair Dye for Light or Dark Colours'; 'Oil of Cantharidin for growth of hair'; 'Curling Fluid'; 'Bloom of Roses for giving beauty to the lips and cheeks'; 'Skin Tightener for furrows'. And look, there's even a nose machine for shaping the nose and an ear machine for outstanding ears. Ah now see, this is more what I need, although the Bloom of Roses sounds tempting, it's Peppers Quinine and Iron Tonic, an English import, which 'Purifies and Enriches the blood and Animates the Spirits and Mental Faculties'. Bottles contain twenty-four doses. In twenty-four doses I could solve the problem of Babette, if she is indeed the patchouli girl.

All that mental diversion and I did not even notice the walk to the Guerbois. I knot my apron behind me and begin clearing some of the tables. Four men rise from the table nearest the large front window so I turn my attention there, lifting glasses and plates. The sight of one large peacock feather balancing on the ashtray gives me pause. I allow myself a smile. My masked man was here. In fact he must have just left this second. Quickly stepping out the door, I watch as a small knot of men cross to the other side of the street. The feather feels soft between my fingers. As I turn to go back inside I see, leaning against the wall with his arms folded and a familiar grin, George, the young failed-painter-turned-writer. I swat him on the cheek with the feather.

'You?'

'Sorry to disappoint, but yes, me.'

'You took your time making yourself known.'

He lifts my hand to his lips. 'I have been flirting madly with you for weeks, but it was getting me nowhere.'

I cannot say that I noticed. Or if I did, I would have banished it as a mere figment of my sometimes nonsensical thought process. Serving him here in this café, it would not have occurred to me that he would even consider conversing with me. When I come here to work I strap on my subservience as I do my apron, and knot it just as tightly, only allowing my mind to be daring. I would need a few doses of Pepper's Quinine and Iron Tonic to unravel this one. Or just let it be as is. But there's the question of Babette, and maybe George can be of help. It would bridge a gap and may prove an interesting diversion. Something to talk over that would not highlight the sheer polarity of our existences. This is Paris, a paint-box, so I should not fret too much.

'The *patron* will be stomping around in there if I don't go back inside, but come to Agnes's café this night at nine. I need your help with something.'

'I'm there.'

George straightens his hat and ambles off. I watch him leave with the swagger of an easy upbringing, the confidence that comes with everything being gifted to you, and an assurance that he wears like a well-fitted coat.

Maman is rocking herself gently on the fireside chair. It is a very slight movement that I try to discourage as the swaying seems to indicate a disconnection from her surroundings. The chair is not a rocking chair, but she rocks all the same. I miss her busyness. I miss the bustling of my childhood memories where the cook was a source of constant disappointment but mother was always able to salvage everything. She felt sorry for the cook because she simply couldn't cook and would never find employment anywhere else. Father would sit with his newspaper in dreaded anticipation of what would be placed each evening before him. Sometimes he would mutter, 'much better tonight', as his plate was collected. This would make the cook feel even worse as it would remind her how unskilled she must normally be. Then father's perceived encouragement spurred her to 'experiment' just to please him even more. This always proved disastrous. There was the time when she learned to cook things in aspic so we had a parade of jellied delicacies, each more unpalatable than the next. I think the jellied pigeons might have been what broke father in the end as he sent the place-setting before him crashing to the ground with one sweep of his arm. Or maybe that was just another excuse to escape down to Marseilles.

Maman gathered up autumn fruits and vast sugary, bubbling cauldrons sweetened the air. She plucked recalcitrant weeds with her long delicate fingers. She planted seeds for spring blossoming. While father would plant soft kisses on her cheek in his comings and goings and I knew, just knew, this was never enough for her. He crushed me in his arms with unbridled joy and I worshipped him. How could my mother not want that love? Being an only child, I presumed that it was because I was so special that she wanted no others.

There must have been a reason why there were no more siblings, but it is never something I discussed with her. What would be the point?

I never liked the old priest in the nearby village as his questioning of my personal development was much too intimate for my liking. He would chastise the women of the district from the pulpit for not being in a permanent state of lactation. They somehow were not fulfilling God's plan if they were not with child year after year until barrenness crept up on them leaving them dry and withered. How joyless, I always thought. Then the old women would gather round and discuss the wandering underused wombs of the women who, like my mother, had underperformed in their heaven-ordained task of procreation. A wandering womb leads to madness, they would say, and the priest would confirm this because, as he often liked to remind us, he spoke Greek. The fact that the Greek word for womb was *hystera*, he pompously declared, is why men never get hysterical and women are practically destined for the condition. As I say, I never liked the man.

My mother is sad and I wish I could brighten her life. I wish I could build a house for her somewhere pleasant with a nice big garden. She used to make me elaborate gingerbread cakes in the style of a Swiss cottage and I would love to build such a cottage for her, with brick up to the first floor and then wood up to the thatched roof with a gleaming white balcony cutting it in two.

'Fleur, I had a dream last night.'

'Yes, *Maman*?'

'I dreamt I was fishing. It was a beautiful clear blue pond and I had a picnic basket and I was sitting on a little canvas stool holding a long rod.'

'That's nice.'

'Yes, but I didn't put any bait on the rod because I didn't want to hurt the fish and I spent hours sitting there, wondering what I was doing, but knowing that if people were looking at me, they would think I was fishing.'

* * *

George surges through the door, unbuttoning his coat as he approaches me and I realise I am stirring my *café* much too vigorously. My cup is in danger of shattering into little pieces.

'How lovely to get you alone, sitting opposite me, instead of you crashing plates of food down in front of me.'

'I would consider myself a very good *serveuse*.'

'Yes, but I can tell by the briskness in your step what kind of mood you are in. Do you know that you walk quicker when you are annoyed? And just occasionally, the tableware suffers for it.'

George orders *un café au lait*, and I begin to relay the tale of the girl I had shared the Spaniard's stairwell and divan with and how worried I am for her safety. George, I feel, is not paying attention.

'You have such a pleasant face.' He is smiling at me as I am trying to infuse my tale with the intensity I truly know it deserves. I chastise him.

'None of that now, we have too much to try to figure out.' He is beautiful. He is tousled as if he has just rolled from his bed and that is where my thoughts are leading me. His smell is of musky decadence, of sheets that have been slept on for several days or rich leather trunks on luxurious train journeys. If I could touch it, his smell would be the sweat-beaded hide of a deer in flight. I am aware he is speaking.

'Does this mean you have cast me in the role of some moustached ploddingly dull police inspector? I protest with every breath in my body. I am a cultured man, a man who at the drop of a hat could recite the names of every Greek and Roman God alphabetically, I might add. Yet you sit there confusing me with someone who would collar a scrawny, lice-infested beggar and take pleasure in it? I am appalled.'

All of this because I have asked for his help.

'My dear George, I know your type. And much as it would shatter you to realise it, you are, my friend, a type. You probably should have become a lawyer, only as you are, no doubt, a younger son, you would have been indulged by an adoring mother and an impatient father. Your studies, though you were more than capable, would have bored you, so at your mother's persuasion, your father, who probably secretly admires your free spirit, decided to fund you while you slipped off into the world to spread your wings. However, in time you will be recalled, and your wings will be clipped, and you will comfortably slip back to your perch, but all the better for having known me and known Paris at this moment.'

There is a brief pause. George raises his glass to his lips while making utterances to no one in particular. 'She called me "dear" and she called me "friend" that, in anyone's book, is a start.'

'Are you going to have time to be able to help me George? In fact, how much work do you have on at the moment?'

'It's building slowly. I had a few poems in the *Chat Noir* newspaper and I wrote several pieces in support of Impressionism. Friends have been telling me to row in behind some sort of movement to have Montmartre declared an independent state, but God knows that would be far too much aggressive anxiety sealed into too small an area. It would quickly implode. You know how precious and neurotic creative types are. No, thank you. And you, Fleur, is clearing tables to be your life?'

It is a little embarrassing. I am eighteen years of age, nearly nineteen, and yes, from whatever angle I may choose to view it, the occupation of table clearing seems to be unfurling well into my future. When would I have had the breathing space to be able to aspire to anything? Only the well-fed can allow themselves that indulgence. And yet I am surrounded in Montmartre by hopeless dreamers, some of whom even got lucky. I know that I am torn between a sense of grinding responsibility and an admiration for the careless.

'I feel fortunate to have a job at all and to be able to pick up the odd sitting along the way.'

'You would make an uninteresting party guest in that case. You need to imagine you are in a room with amusing people and try to decide on what it is you could contribute. It doesn't have to be huge. The most pathetic wordsmith will confidently climb up on stage and think he's Baudelaire and would not be scorned for it. Another may warble a song that only vaguely skirts a recognisable key. We used to sit around our dining table and my father would point at me, or my brothers and sisters, or some poor friend who happened to be there and he would bellow, "Make a statement!" And on the spot you would have to make some pronouncement on politics or the Church or the state of the economy or even the colour of the sky that day. "Make a statement": it's not a bad approach to living.'

'It doesn't sound as if you have a well-thought-out plan of direction either, yet I'm sure deep down, you know much will be expected of you. Do you know where you are going in life?'

'No need to know exactly. Imagine if explorers had actually sailed the right course to India ... America would never have been discovered.'

'Then I declare that my mission is to find Babette, so consider yourself enlisted.'

George smiles and snaps a salute. 'I'll make enquiries.'

* * *

I stop by Maria's on my way home and she beckons me into her cramped one-room apartment. She wipes her hands on an old cloth and steps back from the easel. Staring defiantly at me is a self portrait in pastel that she has been working on. The chin is slightly raised, almost scornfully; the hair severely parted in the middle and tucked behind the ears; the neckline of the dress is conservative and prim. The general effect lacked even a hint of flattery. It was a powerful drawing, bold and unforgiving.

'Maria, that is incredible. I mean as a drawing it is unbeatable. As my beautiful, lively friend on the other hand, you are being unkind to yourself.'

Maria laughs.

'Realistic you mean. I listen to Monet and Renoir and Degas at the Café de la Nouvelle-Athènes and honestly, they would paint my nose and your shoulders and someone else's neck rather than look at any one of us as a whole. So there I am, more than just a composition of elegant body parts belonging to other people.'

She unties the string from a large cardboard folder and spreads out a selection of drawings. Some are of her mother, sitting sternly and glumly. Others are nude self-portraits in charcoal, with strong viscous lines.

'Remember when I used to sit for old Puvis, and he would

turn me into Greek nymphs? Now that required a bit of imagination. He even managed to conjure me up as a scrawny young boy a few times. I have scars on my body from when I used to ride horses, back when I was lithe and acrobatic. It doesn't exactly lend itself to the alabaster look, and yet there I was, marble-like and crowned with eucalyptus leaves.'

'Well lucky you. I once ended up as a gin-soaked spinster, slumped in a darkened alleyway. The very idea!'

Maria bundles up her drawings with the string again and makes two bowls of coffee. 'So tell me about you and the dashing George.'

I glance down and brush some invisible crumbs from my skirt. 'We're on a project together; that is all. And you have not been released from it either.'

Maria clears her throat as if trying to dislodge something while I blow on my coffee with more intensity than the temperature of the coffee demands. I do know that George sees me as more than just a companion. I know by the way he holds my gaze. I know he is trying to decide if I am worth the effort or not.

'Fleur, do you not like him?'

'I have seen dozens of men like George pass through Montmartre. You know there are plenty of unwanted babies belonging to laundry girls and passing students. You know how so many girls have pinned their hopes on these heady romances only to be forgotten once the train pulled away. There is usually a ticket in their pocket and that is what determines how long the relationship will last. What makes you think George is any different?'

'He obviously likes you.'

'Of course he likes me, Maria. He is young and carefree. Liking women is what he does. I know this sounds crude, but I listen to the men in the café and they would put it in anywhere and often times, in anyone, just to be boastful and because it feels good. Thrusting away their ardour with no more thought or care than if they were going for a stroll. Will he fall in love with me? Maybe, and what then? He is going to take a penniless waitress and model home to his big house and wealthy parents? Is that how you see this ending, Maria?'

'Come on Fleur, you've been with other men, often less interesting and definitely not as handsome. Why don't you just enjoy his company, for however long that is?'

'Somehow it would seem harder to do that with George. Look, I've arranged to meet him again at Agnes's café on Wednesday. I can put his brain to use. Will you come? I feel sure that Babette is my patchouli girl. She is uppermost in my mind at the moment. I cannot allow myself to think of George in any other way.'

Maria merely raises an eyebrow and begins to clear the cups away not saying another word. I rub my thighs and try to take a deep breath to compose myself. Kissing Maria on both cheeks, I leave and walk slowly home. I should proceed with more urgency because *Maman* can get disorientated if she has been left alone for a long period of time.

SWEET MEADOW MOIST

I feel a little unseemly loitering in the shadows like this but it is the only way I can watch Fleur's front door. There is a gaiety of purpose amongst all the strollers as they randomly criss-cross the streets and alleys. I am distracted by them and they are blocking my view. Was that a stooped old lady coming out her front door in her bare feet? This isn't right. I strain to see, but she is gone again. No, this is not a good idea. I hoped that if I stopped by here for a little while it might grace me some time before I decide my next move, but standing here in the shadows with my little Japanese-print bag, I know I would just be one more burden for Fleur and her mother. It simply wouldn't be fair. So there is nothing for me but the crumpled address that I kept, the one Cécilia sent to me, as I need somewhere warm and welcoming.

I have enough of a sense of the city to hail an omnibus I know to be travelling in the right direction. The driver reins it to a halt and I climb into it. People are moving along the footpaths in a shimmering distortion as the light from the gas lamps illuminates them on their way and speckles their shadows. As the traffic clatters along, among this ballet of motion, I see one short stout woman in a kerchief, selling something from a basket strapped over her neck. Are they roses? She looks detached. No one is interested, least of all her. Must she come to hate those roses at the end of a long, weary night, and must they come to represent utter defeat and an empty stomach? There is a bundle of blankets in a doorway behind her and something stirs among them. Is it a dog? Is it a child? We trot on.

I double check the address as I stand in front of the low iron gate. There is a small tidy garden and a stone path leading to a Gothic porch, walled on both sides with a pointed-arch entrance. I look for the bell pull. It feels like a lifetime since this morning. I had not realised that in among all those nasty, frustrated nuns, there was indeed a kindly one who made it her personal mission to reunite the young prisoners with their families. She had somehow tracked down and contacted my own family. When I stood before the prefecture's desk and listened in a daze while being told of my release to a family member, I couldn't take it all in. The painter, it seems, was not murdered near his easel but took a tumble down his stairs, probably in a state of drunkenness. The blow to his head must have killed him. I numbly turned to seek out Paulette and then crushed her into a long hug and even cried when it dawned on me that my former tormentor would have to stay behind in her cell. My next shock was seeing my older sister sitting primly on the edge of a chair in one corner of the visitors' room, in a fine hat. The ensuing conversation keeps playing over and over in my brain.

'I had to come in person and sign something to get you out of here, so you are now free. I have decided not to tell mother, and I think it best you stay here in Paris. Papa has been under enormous stress with his business, and he has been advised to take a trip to the seaside for recuperation purposes, otherwise his health will deteriorate. You may come and visit us this summer. My baby is due then, and if I think it suitable, you can live with us and look after your niece or nephew. But only if you do not get into any trouble between now and then.'

I was aware of drawing up to my full length, which is at least a head shorter than my sister and assuring her that I was most grateful for her offer by that I was fortunate to have a few positions to consider in Paris which would keep me well occupied. Not a chance. It is inconceivable that I would remain forever beholden to the 'good' daughter and what-ever future compromises I would undoubtedly find myself enslaved by. As for being a custodian of her offspring … I don't think I'd be able to trust myself. I would probably set about corrupting the cherub as soon as it sprang hollering from her practically virginal loins. We walked through the prison courtyard together and out of the large doors which opened directly on to the street where a carriage was wait-ing. We kissed each other, and I did not wait to see my sister settled in her seat. She didn't protest too much at my deci-sion to stay, and I could just picture her, hands laced together, sighing deeply and assuring herself that, regrettably, she did all she could but that trying to harness my waywardness would be as pointless and elusive as trying to harness the wind.

I crossed the cobbled road on to the pavement, and turned the corner away from the prison in quickening strides, staring straight ahead in case I caught the eye of someone with a remit to send me back inside. My step felt so light it was if I could take flight like a butterfly.

But standing in front of this doorway, I am filled with a foreboding of what will happen if I am allowed across this threshold, and yet also a sense of resignation, a powerlessness which in itself is a relief. Taking a deep breath, I tug at the bell pull and the door is briskly opened. I am presuming this efficiency is somehow to guarantee a degree of discretion for the caller and not have them loitering on the door step for others to take heed. A heavy woman with too much rouge on her cheeks, wearing a crisp white apron stares with a degree of confusion at me.

'Can I help you?' she asks in a very unhelpful tone of voice.

'I'd like to see Mademoiselle Catherine. I am … was … a friend of her cousin Cécilia's.'

'Catherine. Is that what she is known as, or her real name?'

'Her real name, I think, no I'm sure.'

The woman opens the door a crack wider and nods for me to enter. She directs me into a small and neat parlour with several round tables positioned in the corners, all covered in pretty tablecloths. I am instructed to wait. There is one large vase overflowing with fresh flowers. I finger some ornaments above the fireplace and glance at the paintings on the walls, all sensual, coquettish nudes done in the style of Rubens with their apple cheeks and dimpled bottoms. I draw my hands down the fringed poppy-red curtains and hold them briefly against my cheek. It is such a pleasure to feel something soft after the iron and metal-edged prison months. I turn towards the door at the sound of someone clearing her throat and there, I know immediately, is Catherine. Although Cécilia said they were nothing alike, I can see a family resemblance;

Catherine is a taller, more refined version of Cécilia. I find myself looking at her fingers, the fingers that Cécilia so coveted, the slimness of which, in her mind, divided the family into such diverging destinies.

'I didn't catch who you are.'

I stride over to her. 'My name is Babette.' I say this while glancing over Catherine's shoulder to see if anyone could be listening and lower my voice almost to a whisper.

'We, Cécilia and I, met, well, we came across each other at Saint Lazare.' This seems to have concentrated her attention as Catherine closes the door and motions for me to sit down. 'She was a very good friend to me. I miss her. She sent me this address and told me you were here.'

'Is there something wrong with her?'

'Oh I'm so sorry. I thought you would have heard. She's dead.'

Catherine drops her head slightly, then, composing herself again, raises her perfectly arched eyebrows.

'I suppose that was to be expected at some point.'

She stands up from her chair with the same effortless elegance that I witnessed at Madame Gouloumes' Boarding House for Young Ladies. I think you must have to practice this while balancing a book on your head.

'I thank you for telling me this and appreciate you stopping by. I will think fondly of her, poor thing.'

'No, you don't understand. She gave me this address because she believed I would fit in here, that I would find this a suitable place to stay … and …'

'You do know where you are? You know what we do here?'

'Yes, yes. But I have nowhere else to go. When my sister came to claim me from the prison she made it perfectly clear that I wasn't welcome to go home, as I had shamed the family.'

'It is not up to me to let you stay. I shall have to talk to Madame.'

She glides slowly from the room, her skirts barely ruffling. I am suddenly feeling more nervous than I have at any point up to this. I notice a small fly on the wall, and focus all my attention on it remembering the vow I had made to myself. The clock ticks loudly and menacingly, yet I have no sense of how much time has passed when the door opens and a tall lady with a tight glossy chignon and a warm smile enters followed by Catherine.

'Step back a little, girl. Let me look at you.' And so begins a curious stand-off, a mutual appraisal, she of this stranger who has just turned up on her doorstep, me of the type of woman who would run such an establishment. She looks like a youthful aunt, not quite having reached the stage where you kindly describe women of a certain age as 'well preserved'. She does not appear to have to make too much effort in her presentation. I expected someone older and plumper, per-haps swathed in yards of crinoline or, God help us, red satin, with a red cupid-bow lip painted on a white powdered face. I expected garishness, a caricature.

What she thinks of me is hard to judge. I do a small twirl for her as self-consciously as if I were a little girl showing off a new pair of boots. I twirl because it somehow seems expected. Then she does an odd thing – she steps forward and hugs me warmly. My arms dangle awkwardly by my sides. As her embrace softens, I step back.

'My name is Babette, Madame.' She smiles, as if she had been expecting me.

'Thank you, Catherine. You mustn't keep your gentleman waiting.'

Before leaving the room, Catherine gives me a look that is hard to determine. Was it scorn? Perhaps jealousy? I can see a young man loitering in the hallway holding his hat in his hands. Madame gestures for me to sit down.

'How old are you now, Babette?'

'Sixteen, Madame. Seventeen in a matter of days.'

'And you think you want this life? Do you realise that this is a path which once committed to, is impossible to veer from? That you are unlikely to be able to mix in respectable company without the constant worry you will be unearthed? That it is unlikely you will ever find a husband?'

'I have given this some thought.' This was an outright fib because I have given it barely any thought at all, except that I considered it a preferable alternative to living in disgrace with my sister. And truthfully, if that sweet Fleur girl was living in any better circumstances, I would have prevailed upon her for a little while. Besides, I am ruined already and I just feel so tired that I cannot even think straight.

'Have you no family that perhaps would be in a position to talk you out of this?'

'Madame, I am alone here.'

'Well, if you work hard, you will be able to look after yourself as you get older.' The Madame rang a bell and the heavy lady who had first answered the door came into the room. 'Hélène, find Babette some outfits. I think that lavender dress would be lovely on her.' Madame takes hold of both of my shoulders. 'We are a girl down, so there is room for you here. We will have to get you registered with the prefecture, but beyond that, there should be no concerns.'

I feel a wave of relief that I am entrusted to something where any decision making has been removed from me. This is soon followed by an even stronger sense of dread.

* * *

I am again sitting on the edge of my bed waiting. It has been several days now since I unpacked and so far I have not received the warmest of welcomes from the other girls. Catherine had done little to make me feel wanted, and only that it isn't her place to do so, I feel sure that given half a chance, she would have me tossed out on to the street. I spend my days pruning and preening. The knock on the door is purposeful and sure enough, Madame Del bustles in, followed by Hélène who is carrying a dress, a floaty delicacy cushioned against her puckered plump arms. It is white chiffon with a black lace insertion and embroidered cuffs and collar. Madame reaches above the tall wardrobe and takes hold of one of the hatboxes. She pulls out a bonnet in white muslin decorated with silk bows. Then from a drawer Madame lifts out a strange rough-looking cushion made from straw and places it alongside the dress on the bed.

'Your first guest this evening, Babette, will be Dr Philippe. He was a very important man in the court of Napoleon the third. Hélène will prepare your clothes, then help you dress.'

'What, Madame, is this?'

'This particular gentleman is partial to large bustles, and it's important to accommodate our guests' taste. Sometimes he wants his girls in walking dresses and other times in evening dress. He has requested our newest girl for this evening. Now, for your undergarments, you are to wear your camisole attached to the knee-length drawers and that white petticoat. But you are to wear split drawers.'

Madame Del primly nods.

'Go to the kitchen and get yourself a very light supper. We don't want you chaffing against your corset. Hélène has a bit of sewing to do.'

I try to nibble a little food but find it physically impossible to do so. I allow myself to be dressed, raising my arms at Hélène's direction, lifting my legs when I feel a tap at my ankles. I am yanked back like a naughty puppy on a leash as Hélène's meaty arms tug at my corset stays. I flatten the ruffles around my collar and take small steps around the room while glancing over my shoulders. The steel half-hoops in the skirt lining give my dress a life of its own. Examining myself in a long mirror I am disappointed to see that my complexion is still that of someone who has not seen the light of day for a long time.

'Hélène, don't you think I look a little like the hind legs of a horse in this?'

'You look as you look. It's not for you to judge.'

Madame enters the room again and, after smoothing out the ribbons on the bonnet and adjusting my posture slightly, she indicates that I should follow her. This bustle feels very large and I have to swing my way forward which must make me look like an undulating camel trying to cross the Sahara. Whatever do men find appealing about this? I try not to look at the floor. Madame Del wafts into a large room, one I had never been in before. Her gestures are more theatrical now and she has an extravagant greeting for the man in the top hat who is standing very tall and straight by the fireplace. He takes her hand and kisses it.

'Dr Philippe, this is our lovely Lily.'

I don't know when the decision to change my name was made, but approaching this man as Lily seems a lot easier than as Babette.

'Dr Philippe, delighted to meet you.' I try to outdo Madame in the extravagance of my gestures, but can immediately tell by the faint crease on her brow that my enthusiasm may need a little reining in. I take a seat at the other side of the fireplace while Madame Del nods and leaves the room. As he looks to place his hat on a table, I shoot a studying glance at the caller, being careful not to ogle. He is thin with an untidy grey beard and heavy eyebrows. He looks like the bony type that would sit in his library and summon his grandchildren one by one to test them on their knowledge of geography. His eyes are slate coloured and his cheeks slightly flushed. He crosses his long legs and, with his elbows perched on the well-stuffed arm rests, he forms a pyramid shape with his fingertips and taps his lips. Who is meant to speak first?

This room is very different from the parlour that I was first brought in to. There is an overcrowding of ornamentation. A large round table sweeps up through the throats of two white carved swans and they in turn are entangled in gilt-edged lilies and bulrushes. A white and gold bookcase is carved on either side with two boys in curls and arms crossed over their chests, ensnared by gold leaves. The room is warmed by the fire and half lit from the dimmed lamps. The chair that the good doctor is relaxing in is stuffed and plump, while the one that I am perched on would be better placed in a church. My fingers toy with diminutive flying buttresses on the wooden armrests. I feel that if I lay my head back, my hair would get caught up in the profusion of turrets that are carved at every angle. I must appear to him as if I am wearing a mitre as the back of my chair looms into an elaborate pinnacle jutting towards the ceiling high above my hat. Everything is sharp and angular and unless I remain perfectly still, I fear I may do myself an injury. I notice that there is a silver tea and coffee service laid out all punched with the designs of what looks to be Chinese men, I expect in the process of bartering their wares. I rise.

'Shall I pour you some tea or would you prefer some coffee, Monsieur?'

He uncrosses his legs and pats his thighs. 'I want you to come and sit here on my lap.'

I feel as if I could snap off this ridiculously decorated handle and I crash the pot back down on to the tray, turning to him in fury. I am sure I would scarcely be able to tell the difference between sitting on his lap and sitting on that angular church chair.

'You, Monsieur, are a very crude man. If I was on the street, you would at least have to engage me in some initial small talk. The elegance of these surroundings highlights you to be as much out of place as a pig in a parlour.'

As I stomp towards the door, I manage, to my surprise, to get some fluidity into my cumbersome garments.

'I believe Monsieur or Doctor, you have the wrong address and perhaps you should try the Place de Pigalle. You would find that more to your liking, or more accurately, to your style. And I don't care if you knew Napoleon.'

Brushing passed Madame Del in the hallway and carrying the weight of dress as I make my way back upstairs, to my extreme annoyance, I can hear the man's laughter rolling out from the front room. I manage to step out of these clothes much quicker that I was layered into them. Madame Del knocks and enters, telling me to sit down. I throw my bonnet on to the bed with an alarmingly instinctive display of petulance and sit with my arms crossed. I know that I am going to be told I do not have 'what it takes' and will be marched out the front door. Madame Del remains standing with her hands clasped in front of her

'You see, this is the problem with taking in girls who have not been vouched for. Babette, this is a business, my business. I look at you now, and my feeling is that you need not begin this life in earnest at all. I think you should pack up your belongings and go find another job. I'm sure there are plenty things you would like to do? Be a seamstress, or a shop girl. You could take your chances like the hundreds of other girls who come to this town looking to make a better life. You could model again.'

My shoulders sink a little.

'Or you could choose to make your trades wisely. We all give up something to gain something. What I can offer you here is cultured company that will treat you well. You can be the mistress of a wealthy, educated man and as many other men as you wish or you could be the companion of an impoverished person of worthy virtue. You could throw your lot in with someone who love romantically yet have that strangled to death through the sheer grind of making ends meet. Or you could live a life of refinement and ease. I can't make that choice for you, Babette. Of course, it's always possible that you could walk out this gate and meet the perfect person in the best of circumstances and live happily from here on in. I don't want to deny you that if you believe that to be possible. You have your beauty, Babette, which places you in a better than average position.' Madame Del steps over to me and smoothes my carefully frizzed fringe. 'Look at you. All grown up but still like a delicate flower.'

She softly exits the room, leaving me alone sitting on my bed. I take a few seconds to compose myself then begin gathering up my belongings. I pull my Japanese-print bag out from under my bed and begin to place my things into it. Snapping it closed I take one long look at it. All my worldly belongings amount to one small bulge. Looking around at the plump cushions, the upholstered chairs, the wardrobe of dresses, the stack of hat boxes, even the small plate of *madelines* that have been left out for me to eat when I fancied, I revise my decision. As an already fallen woman, my options are severely limited, so better to lead a life of vice in refined surroundings than to take my chances on my own, in a city where I haven't had the best of fortune so far. Then there is my sister's proposition, but even the thought of that is making my chest constrict. I leave my room and call for Madame Del from the top of the staircase. She appears almost instantly at the foot of the stairs.

'Madame, I've decided to stay.'

Madame Del smiles and nods.

'Very good. Now, in future do not stand half dressed at the top of my staircase. You want to make the caller feel he has to try just a little.'

* * *

Brushing my hair in my room and thinking of nothing in particular Hélène is suddenly at my side, placing a compact dark-red velvet box in front of me. She leaves without giving an explanation. I caress it before snapping it open. Tucked among the folds of silk is a sparkling diamond bracelet. There is also an embossed card.

Mlle Lily,

Please allow this trinket to represent in some small way, a token of my regret for my boorish behaviour on our first meeting. If I have not wounded you too deeply, I would be most pleased if you would wear it while accompanying me this Friday to the Opéra Comique.

P.

Clasping the bracelet onto my wrist, somehow the prison pallor of my skin seems less noticeable. I am sure I should feel something even mildly bordering on indignation or shame. But this bracelet immediately looks as if it belongs on my wrist and I instantly feel as if I am entitled to be wearing it. Have I so easily crossed into this world of commerce where I can now be valued in the cut of a diamond? Assessing my outstretched hand as my bracelet winks in ice-blue sparkles, my answer appears very quickly and unashamedly to be, 'Yes!'

* * *

Madame Del chooses the dress I am to wear. It is shimmering pale pink and sleeveless with a lower neckline than anything I have ever worn before. She warns me that the scent I am wearing is far too strong and that I must go for something more delicate, with violet, lavender or rose notes. Babette likes patchouli, but I understand Lily should wear, well, something like lily. There are two bottles on my dressing table, one squat with a fat glass stopper, the other long necked. I circle the long-necked bottle under my nose, then the squat one. The squat one reminds me of helping my mother to bake, then sitting with my elbows on the wooden table waiting with a knife to slice into the sweet springy moistness. It is a smell of burnt sugar and caramel with hints of vanilla. I dismiss it as it reminds me too much of home. The longer bottle is more what Lily should wear. It is a wild-flower meadow after a short cloudburst of spring showers. More a lilt than a chorus; it is only apparent if you were to brush someone close by. It is a whispered secret. This is Lily's scent.

A carriage pulls up at the garden gate and on the seat is a mixed bouquet with a note telling me I will be met on arrival. True to his word, there stands Philippe, leaning against one of the enormous columns that frame the grand entrance.

Five steps bring me to where he waits with his elbow cocked for me to link on to him. We step into the large entrance hall and with several nods of his head to lustrous men and women on both his right and left, we fall into a swell of black tails and taffeta ruffles as it slowly surges up the gleaming staircase. The wave parts and we are ushered into a private box with its own balcony. There is red velvet everywhere and as I take my seat, I suddenly feel like a jewel in a jewellery box. And so begins a night that is a whirl of sensations, as if I was being sweetly caressed with feathers. I feel sure no better introduction to opera could have been conceived.

'*Lakmé,*' Philippe informs me in whispered tones once the prelude about to strike up, 'is both beautiful and tragic. Léo Delibes created the role for an American singer called Marie van Zandt. You will see her very early on in the first act. To my mind, the first thing to savour is the duet between Lakmé and her servant, Mallika, the "Flower Duet", but throughout, the orchestration is delicate and teasing. You will love it.'

I watch transfixed as the stage becomes a holy place where the Hindus perform their mysterious rites under the high priest, while the beautiful Lakmé and her servant go down to the river, where Lakmé removes her jewellery and they set off to gather flowers. As their duet soars and swoops to the final chorus, '*Sous le dôme épais ou le blanc jasmine. Ah! Descendons, ensembles!*' I feel sure my heart will burst from my chest. How can something so beautiful be so discomforting? And in this instant, I suddenly feel as if I have matured into a proper woman. There is a pleasure-pain continuum that my younger untutored self would have scoffed at, the drama of broken hearts and loves won and lost and a sudden aware-ness of the blinding spell that some women can cast on men. How easy it would be to be cruel. The riveting crescendo from this stage has enchanted me into a vulnerable state of whimpering adoration, and I feel powerless.

'If you are feeling a little teary over some white jasmine, Lily, then I shall have to carry you out of here as the love story unfolds between Lakmé and the British Army officer.'

I lean as far forward as I dare, without actually resting my arms on the velvet balcony in front of me, the way a farmer would in surveillance of his sheep, and it keeps me enthralled as the officer first sees Lakmé, which frightens her into crying out for help. She instead turns away her rescuers, indecision I can well relate to. Are others as moved and intrigued as I, or are they much more jaded and less impressed? Perhaps in this distinguished audience, I may well be the only person who is here for the first time. I try to see if there is any other person with the same degree of uncouthness in the matter of all things operatic but there seems little evidence of it. Our balcony abuts another to the right where three young men have an air of distraction. They are being tended to by a white-gloved man who fusses intermittently about them, topping up Champagne flutes. Why is there no lady to accompany even one of them? The man seated in the middle has glanced over in the direction of our box several times now. I really must learn the skill of the subtle side-glance that I am aware other women effortlessly employ. But I find myself matching his boldness. How dare he stare so impertinently? It is because he is aware of his good looks, I am sure.

Philippe has been kind and attentive throughout the performance, prompting me when a scene is about to become tragic as in the third act where Lakmé realises she has lost her love and, rather than live without him, kills herself by eating the poisonous datura leaf. I am aware of Philippe smiling indulgently across at me as I'm sure the expression on my face is altering with the arc of the story until the rousing finale has left me quite drained.

After the opera there is a lively congregation at a small bistro. We join a group of people that Philippe seems to know well. A chair is pulled out for me and I drink whatever is offered to me. No one seems to take much notice of my presence nor is anyone inclined to comment on the very obvious age difference between Philippe and me. I do sense some hostility from another young woman at the far end of the table, who, up to that point, must have been the centre of attention with her corn blonde hair and fluttering eyes. Though I feel over-dressed, this must be all part of the theatre ritual: first to soak in the atmosphere of opulence then afterwards, to come to a place like this for banter and cognac. The owner sends more drinks over, while expressing his huge relief that he has customers who will settle with actual money at the end of the night and that he has an attic full of bad paintings as a testament to customers who don't. Philippe points towards the bearded gentleman sitting up front by the window.

'You will probably notice that man, Monsieur Degas, hanging about theatres we may go to. He likes to paint the dancers and seems to be quite revered among the other painters, from what I hear.'

I am caught between the pleasing acknowledgments that there will be more outings such as this and my observation of how very morose Monsieur Degas looks.

It is very late when I bustle back into Madame's house. Glancing into the small parlour, I see Catherine sitting by the fire, reading a letter. I'm glad she is there because I am overflowing with excitement and eager to describe the night, detail by very small detail. I flop on the fireside chair opposite Catherine, released of the duty of deportment.

'Catherine, such a wonderful night. I think I shall love opera forever. Have you been to many? I was actually very nervous because I didn't know how to act and I didn't want to appear foolish.'

Catherine lets out an irritated sigh.

'Catherine do you still have some sort of problem with me?'

She crashes her letter back down on to her lap in crumpled frustration.

'Babette, for heaven's sake. Everything does not have to be all about you, all of the time. You are like something hopping up and down, craving attention.'

'Well I am very sorry, but this happens to be all very new to me.' I straighten myself in the chair and am about to launch a further point of defence when I notice one slow tear tracing an outline down her cheek.

'Catherine, is everything all right?' She doesn't speak, but smoothes the letter out on her thigh to re-read it. 'Is it a love letter?' She nods. I crouch down in front of her. 'If I made you some hot chocolate, would that make you feel a little better?' That cheers her up a little.

'You know, Catherine, you reminded me a little there of your cousin, Cécilia.'

Right. To the kitchen. Is there anyone up who can make us some hot chocolate or will I have to do it myself? I quite like the way this dress swishes.

EARTHY DAMP

It does surprise me sometimes how women such as Maria, Agnes and I can distract ourselves for inordinate amounts of time in lovingly overturning mere trivia; how we can move from a forensic analysis of the best way to keep our cuticles neatly scraped back, to the mocking of the drunken gait of a passing gentleman and the likelihood his tumbling, how there is a very good selection of brocaded velvets and fancy velvets as well as marked-down lingerie for sale at Le Bon Marché, to the merits of drinking cold black coffee with seltzer water. When George arrives, his presence immediately draws our conversation away from these minutiae. I think it is simply his masculinity. He pulls up a chair and we instinctively turn towards him as if we were three sunflowers reaching for the light.

'We're here to find Babette.' I say this in what amounts to a command, to distance ourselves from the disparate frivolity of our earlier chattering. In truth, the search has become part of a ruse to be able to remain in George's company. But it is a useful one, and I have convinced myself that the patchouli girl and Babette are one and the same. Agnes leaves us to attend to the kitchen. George flicks open his moleskin notebook and thumbs the pages back and forth, while Maria recalls the information she managed to tease out of the haughty young art student.

'Well that ties in, because judging by the date that you say the girl was arrested, she must have been linked to the death of the Spaniard. From what I remember hearing, he owed a lot of people money.'

'He had that reputation, but he always paid me, probably not wanting to be beholden to a model, although scruples tended not to be too high up on his agenda from the stories that are being told about him.'

'Yes but what artist doesn't owe somebody somewhere money?' George is very familiar with their habits.

Maria looks at both of us.

'What, so are we just presuming she didn't do it?'

'Well I won't know for sure until I talk to her, until I can ask her.'

George again flips through a couple of pages.

'You know there are a few prisons here, don't you? But women are generally sent to the Saint Lazare Prison. Or, and you have to think about this: if she did go mad and kill some-one, then maybe she ended up in Charenton, the asylum.'

This wouldn't bear thinking about. Maria pours some more wine.

'Listen Fleur, you have absolutely no idea what you are getting into here. She is not your responsibility at all. I really think you should let things be. You have enough on your plate with your mother getting worse and you trying to make ends meet.'

'Maria could be right.'

'If I could just talk to her once, I'm sure then I'd know.'

'Well, if you are going to go trawling through prisons, Fleur, you're on your own.'

I am taken aback by Maria's cold tone.

'What? You think I'm being cruel? I never told you this before …' Maria glances quickly at George and then drops her eyes. 'Never mind.'

'Maria, you can trust George. Can't she George?'

George gives a little shrug, as if he doesn't care one way or the other, his empty glass being his only concern. He pours himself more wine.

'Well, my mother was married once, and I have a half-sister. *Maman*'s husband was a blacksmith, a perfectly respectable job, but it wasn't enough for him, so he began to develop skills as a forger. He can't have been very good because he was arrested and then sentenced to a life of hard labour in French Guiana. He died in prison two years later. My older sister was around six when my mother fell pregnant with me. I have no idea who my father was, but he can't have been very decent if he abandoned a widow woman with two small girls. I don't care who he is either.'

'You have a sister?'

'Half of one. She's a respectable married lady somewhere. Anyway, why are you so focused on this? You saw this girl only a handful of times. She could have any number of people in her life.'

Why indeed? It is not merely an excuse to make myself more interesting to George, there is much more to it than that. I still have those memories, as sharp as a whip lash, of being alone in this city. Everybody needs someone. Maria herself had her uncle at the circus. Sometimes it's just the resounding echo of another person bouncing off you to remind you that you are alive. Something in my gut, my very innards, is telling me to find Babette, to make sure she is all right. Maria takes the ensuing pause as somehow an agreement and so continues.

'I just think you could be spending your time more wisely than getting acquainted with a prison.'

'Maria, if Fleur wants to do this, it's her choice. It might seem a little obsessive, but that's fine. I won't hold that against her.'

'No, I suspect there are other things you would rather hold against her.'

I bang the table. 'Enough. You think this is some whimsy of mine? A game? Are you forgetting how tough it is out there? You George, well you can be forgiven, but Maria ... is your memory so short?'

George's neck reddens slightly as points his finger at me.

'Now that's not fair.'

I rock a little in my chair, saying nothing. I do this sometimes as I find it comforting. I know that there is something I must reveal to them. Finishing my wine in one gulp, I draw myself up and speak in as clear and direct voice as I can muster.

'Will you both come with me?'

George and Maria look at each other and nod in perplexed agreement. They say goodbye to Agnes who's been hovering nearby. The streets are getting busy with the early evening pedestrians. We jump on board an omnibus until we reach the market at Les Halles and from there, we walk to the corner of Rue Saint Denis. I creak open the iron gate in the shadow of the neatly walled-off cemetery. Gravel crunches underfoot as George and Maria follow me to a small mound with a posy of fresh flowers placed on top.

'This is my daughter Isobel.'

Maria steps forward and hooks on to my arm saying nothing. We both stare down at the mound of earth. George remains slightly back.

'It was a long time ago.'

The weeds are untamed and I kneel down to pluck at them

'My early days in Paris are a blur. A blur of working like a dog in the house of a distant relative; of brandy-reeking breath and bed-covers being pulled from me; of chairs up against the knob of my bedroom door; of packing up my few things and running away. Not yet fifteen and in the middle of Paris with nowhere to go. I begged a little and stole from vegetable stalls and slept in doorways. I was then given shelter by a man who claimed his entitlements. The day I realised I must be pregnant, I sat on some church steps and rocked and cried and thought I should just throw myself down the steep stairs and be done with it.'

I am aware of George scuffing at the gravel with his boot, as if unsure as to what he should be doing. I sit back on my heels.

'And then this amazing thing, I heard a kind voice, a woman asking me if I was all right. I must have thought she was an angel or something. She was wearing this beautiful cream velvet coat and matching hat, and she smelt of damask roses.'

Maria crouches down beside me and begins to finger for weeds as well.

'She asked about my mother. When she realised I was alone, she told me to follow her because I could be arrested for vagrancy.'

Each time I pull the weeds from this little grave I find my mind drifting to that door beside a bakeshop, to the upstairs parlour room which was so warm with a gloriously blazing fire, to the sensation of water being poured from a jug and my back being gently sponged, my hair being washed and the smell of crisp fresh linen against my tired skin, and of sleeping as if I had a whole life of sleep to catch up on. I reposition the small posy.

'Delphine cared for me over the next seven months or so. I loved that place.' I have a clear vision of her neat little home. 'She had a dresser stacked with fine china and there were delicate, lace tablecloths on all the small tables. She even had a piano. She would barely let me out of her sight, and I always had to walk apart from her if we were out in public. Do you know what the vile book is George?'

George shakes his head as I rise to my feet again.

'Delphine, at great personal risk, made sure I would never end up in it. She was registered as a prostitute. She knew that as an unaccompanied minor in this world, I could be arrested and dumped in the House of Correction, and she could get into trouble for corrupting a minor, just by keeping me with her. It became her personal mission to stop me from ever getting registered, which she feared would be my fate. You know, for that brief time, I could actually imagine living forever with my baby and Delphine, all together in her little home, Delphine like a kindly aunt. I had no fear when I was there.' I feel the need to rock again.

'Isobel was born too early. She only lived for an hour, but oh, she was beautiful. I dressed her in a little lace gown that I had carefully sewn and a little bonnet that was far too big for her, and I wrapped her in a soft woollen blanket. When I had her dressed, Delphine and I brought her here to be buried. I wanted to bury her over there, where respectable people are with their big tombs and all that prayerful respect. Instead, this scrubby field is as near as I could get.'

This field is filled with odd-shaped mounds, formed by desperate hands and dirty fingernails many under the cover of darkness.

'Isobel would have been four on her next birthday.' Right this minute, I can imagine my four-year-old girl dancing around, giggling, and maybe twirling her hair. 'I come here often. I have to. There are stray goats, look, there's one over there now, and they would trample her. At least I can try to protect her from that.' I fill my lungs with one deep breath. 'It's just that I still have this … this ache in my heart. I can still feel that day, still feel the cloth that I folded over her little face before I put her in the ground. There are many things that seem to have fled my mind, many spaces that have been created, but this …'

The memory of that day is whipping me into submission. Poor Maria and George, I have bonded them to my distress. This is what is most difficult when you cast out something heartfelt, you entangle others.

'So there you have it. My baby in a pauper's grave.'

I feel George's hand on my shoulder and it stills me. I remember the torturous decision I made to leave Delphine. It was as foreign and unwelcome as if I was being asked to plunge my hand into boiling water. Every inch of my being recoiled from it, but I knew I had to leave as it wouldn't have been fair on her. She had been so good to me. She started me working with the *patron* at the café. She told me I was always welcome back to her if I ever got into difficulties again, but hoped she would never have to see me. My mother came to Paris shortly after that, totally oblivious, and with her own distress as carefully packed as the small suitcases she carried.

It is beginning to rain and heavy drops start to batter the little bunch of flowers. George unbuttons his coat and throws it over my head for I feel strangely rooted and unable to move.

'Come on. Let's get out of the rain. Maria, squeeze in here as well.'

We all try to run out through the gate together under George's coat and suddenly life seems funny again, as we fall, dripping wet into the nearest doorway for shelter. George reaches across and clasps my hand.

'Listen, I understand. I'll keep making enquiries. I've covered a few of the court sessions. We'll see what we can follow up. I promise you, we'll find Babette.'

* * *

Why do I come back here and torture myself? My hair is now a cloying web encasing my face as the rain stabs me relentlessly. Damp mud has seeped through several layers of my clothing and yet here I kneel, clearing away some leaves from Isobel's grave. I remember leaving with Maria and George and it has happened again … I find my way back here, as if in a trance.

'Fleur.' The voice is like a caress. I look up and it is Agnes, the elegant Madame Vignon. She parts the soggy tresses away from my face with her gloved hands. 'I thought you might be here. Come with me, and we'll get you some nice warm soup.'

There is a small hoof mark left in the gravel and I must fill it in. 'I can't. Look you see, the goat is back.'

Agnes picks up a stone and throws it off into the darkness, towards nothing in particular. 'There. It's gone now.'

And I believe her. I stand and allow her to lead me away. I try not to glance over my shoulder to where my daughter lays. I focus solely on the warm comforting feeling of Agnes's glove against my chapped palm, as she leads me through the crowds to her apartment. I only begin to blink into awareness when I find myself sitting in a large leather chair by the fire, wrapped in a warm shawl with a bowl of soup on my lap.

'I'm not sure why it happened again, Agnes.'

'You must be under some sort of stress.'

Stress: what a baffling thing that is. It alights on you and inhabits you and ultimately debilitates you. Sometimes you are not even aware of its presence until you realise you cannot account for a period of time. I seem to have lost some nights. I stroke my soft stomach.

'Am I trying to destroy myself just so that I can forget there was once a heartbeat here, inside of me, Agnes?'

'Grief dislodges people. You know that. I know that. Our minds become fragile with the burden of having to carry around too many difficulties. That's all. People make much too much of a fuss about it all.'

I watch Agnes as she fastens one of the tiny mother-of-pearl buttons on the cuff of her white blouse. It makes me smile as it reminds me of a gown she used to wear. We both used to wear.

'So declares the, *Fleeing Woman in White*.'

'Yes, well, that was a ridiculous amount of fuss too.'

I did not, for one second, consider what I experienced to be a mental breakdown, even as I was being led with anger rising in my throat, through the gates of the asylum. I had been through the trauma of losing my baby. As far as I was concerned, my reactions were that of a normal person reacting to an abnormal occurrence. If only people had stopped and talked to me about it. I would never have harmed any of those babies that I lifted from the perambulators. I just wanted to clutch them tight into me, to nuzzle them and smell them. That was all. If the smell of a baby was a colour, it would be pink.

I did find it peaceful there though, caught up in the swell of routine beyond the high stone walls. I was astonished to find out, very quickly, that the subject of *Fleeing Woman in White* was a fellow inmate. I had heard the painting being spoken of in tones of admiration, with many rumours circulating about who the ethereal figure in the painting could be. I also had the pleasure of seeing the painting at a retrospective portrait exhibition. It had been around for twenty years or so, dating from the time of Agnes Vignon's first committal to that very institution, as I was to find out through dogged probing.

The story was told that a beautiful woman in a white gown unwittingly became the subject of a renowned painting as she tried to escape. Some bleary-eyed painters were said to have been meandering home when they were astonished to come across a confused woman with fiery hair who stopped like a frightened deer caught in a lamp light, then leaped off through the field, a hint of her long white legs illuminated by the moon. She was, of course, caught, but she had left enough of an impression that her laudanum-fuelled hysteria would be forever framed and perused with casual interest by waves of strangers. I was one of the few people who knew the true identity of the *Fleeing Woman in White*.

'Do you know when I first saw that painting of me, Fleur? It was at the Salon des Refuses around 1863, when I went to track down the portrait that had so dislodged my father. There she was, *Red Hair, White Dress* and as I continued scanning the walls, taking in the other works, there I was too, frozen in my fevered state of mind for time immemorial.'

'You have to admit, it is a stunning painting though.'

'Yes, but really, I'd much rather be sitting on a velvet divan in my favourite hat in some well-appointed room somewhere. I hate to shatter the myth; it does seem the stuff of melodrama, but I'm sure I was just going for a moon-lit walk, rather than actually trying to escape. I suppose it's more than possible that someone did see me. Whether it was the artist himself, I don't know, but I think the story became such a part of the painting that it almost grew to be more significant than it. I'd blame the fevered imagination of the artist myself. They are all such storytellers. There are probably fleeing women in England and Italy, everywhere. I'm sure I wasn't the first mad person to want to absent themselves from an asylum for a harmless stroll.'

'I never considered you mad, Agnes, either in Sainte-Anne's or out of it.'

'It was decided that I drank too much for my own good which meant I exhibited "abnormal impulses". And, because I was fond of men, that meant I was also deemed to be devoid of moral sense.'

'The word "degenerate" was used to describe me.'

'All nonsense.'

'I was grateful for my madness. It protected me.'

'Yes, but you don't want to go back there. This episode is like a carriage wheel that veered slightly out of its rut. Take the reins firmly Fleur. Don't mind these past few days. They are lost so there is no point in fretting about them.'

'This hasn't been the only one of late. A night here and few days there.'

'Fleur, grief can derail people completely. But to be so grief-stricken, well, it's like having an insufficient love of life. You're too young to live in such a state of anxiety. It has taken me a long time. I'm nearly forty now, but I became tired of feeling so displaced that I eventually decided my best defence was to love life.'

I sip at my soup again. Nobody could ever accuse Madame Vignon of not loving life.

'My other piece of advice, from hard-earned experience, is to stay away from artists. Enjoy their company, by all means, and of course their talent, and don't let it stop you working for them, but at the core of an artist is aloofness. This is what enables them to depict what is around them. They have to be aloof in order to create. I am endlessly fascinated by them and envious of their self-absorption but would warn any girl against emotionally investing in them.'

'What about writers?'

'Another story, my dear. I am not going to advise you on what to do about George. I am very, very fond of him, but would I broker a relationship between you two?'

'No, I was just thinking in general.'

She flashes me a knowing smile. 'Rest here tonight.'

Rest. What a beautiful word, a beautiful concept. But my mother needs me. I immediately pull the shawl from around my shoulders. My poor mother, how could I be so inattentive? I hope the *ragoûts* has held out and I do know that she has plenty of mending that will be keeping her busy.

'Thank you so much, Agnes. I'll try not to put you through all of this again.' She takes the shawl from me.

'If you do, you do. But I'd rather you didn't, for your sake.'

* * *

I don't think my absence was necessarily the cause, but there is a dullness about *Maman*, a tiredness and an air of defeat, which I am finding exhausting. I try to maintain a degree of levity because with her every sigh, she seems to be sucking energy from the very air we breathe. It feels as if there is a limited supply of oxygen between us and *Maman* is requiring most of it just to enable her to rise in the mornings. This then is leaving me gasping. I feel she is drawing too much from me, too much from what is ours that is shared.

I have taken to patting Babette's velvet hat on my lap as if it was a loyal cat. I find it soothes me as I conjure up possible scenarios for where she is and what she could be doing that very minute. The faint hint of patchouli always inhabits me long after I have carefully placed the hat back on my small dressing table. The little bird brings with it just enough whimsy to stop me from feeling terribly sorry for myself, reminding me that life is not all grim. Why then would I agree to accompany Maria to a funeral this morning? I suppose in their own way, they can be spectacles and we expect that Manet's will be well attended. Maria pushes me through the crowd so that we can sit on a wall, giving us a clear view of Manet's coffin as it is carried to the cemetery. The crowd of men closes in around the coffin. People often become more boisterous relative to their proximity to a corpse. I think it is a supreme act of denial – as if their laughter and chatter will act as a protective shield and death will become distracted and not seek out another body, at least not yet.

'There goes my initial inspiration. To dust.'

Maria thumps her chest in mock piety.

'But my pledge is not to bury that inspiration like poor Manet is being buried now.'

'I didn't know you knew Manet that well.'

'I always had a tender spot for him. That café of yours, the Guerbois, that's where I first spied him. He used to often sit at a table by the front window, impeccably turned out when I was this runny-nosed scamp peering through the glass. He sat with the same group of men and little did I think then that I'd end up modelling for a few of them.'

'Well I'm sure if they looked out the window and saw this grubby creature staring back, in their wildest dreams, they wouldn't have imagined they'd end up painting you!'

'Renoir was there and Degas, he was one of them too. See those two pallbearers at the rear, Monet and Zola? I remember them being there.'

How strange to bury people in spring; it just doesn't seem right. Everything is bursting forth with new life and new brilliance. You would reasonably expect a morbid scene such as the lowering of a coffin to be dipped in hues of grey. But then Manet, who died such a miserable death, with his gangrenous amputated foot, would probably prefer this to be a colourful occasion. His friends here will probably sign his funeral book and then commit the scene to canvas. Nothing seems private to them. I am trying not to think about my mother. I am trying not to wonder what, if anything, I can do to help her. I am trying not to let my mind drift to the Petites Maisons where poor women are treated, mainly for syphilis.

'Come on. I feel I've done my duty now.'

Maria jumps down from the wall, and I slide to the ground after her, managing to scrape myself in the process whereas she just has to contend with some dirt that can be easily wiped off her dress.

'We'll go look at that statue's head in the park.'

The statue is the talk of Paris; a giant monstrosity of a thing that is to be a gift to the United States of America when it's finished. '*Statue de la Liberté.*' At the moment it is just a huge, decapitated head jutting several storeys high among the blooms of the park. We need to stand quite far back to take in the giant copper face and pointed crown. The lips alone look to be about three feet wide. Maria climbs up onto the platform which holds the huge head. She tries to reach up to the copper chin. She caresses the mottled surface. It seems like an act of pagan worship.

'I could do with this woman's strength. They buried Manet, but long live this goddess of liberty. She will become my new source of inspiration.' Suddenly Maria has a dizzy spell and stumbles.

'Are you all right?'

'I'm fine. Just pregnant.'

'What? When did you find out?' I look around for somewhere to take a seat.

'Don't worry about it. In front of this grand lady, I am vowing not to allow this to oppress or enslave me.'

'How far along are you? Who is the father?'

'I don't know what to tell you. It was one of those nights that started off in gaiety, and then as the night wore on … well, you know, how sometimes, with absinthe, you seem to lose the power of your legs? You know when your mind is fine, but you're getting numb from the toes up and by the time your brain tells you you've drunk too much, well your body is already on the floor?'

'What then?'

Maria looks unconcerned, or making a very good attempt at feigning it.

'That is the problem, I'm not exactly sure. Henri was with me at one point, but my last memory of him is sitting like a crumpled doll on a bench. I remember wild dancing. I remember hands. I woke up in the apartment of some insurance clerk. Fleur, I've no idea if he is the father or not. What was I doing with him of all people? He is so dull and grey, and he does that thing with his nose ... he presses in one nostril and honks. I think it's a mucus problem.'

I can't help myself and begin to laugh. I hold Maria's cheeks between my hands. 'Whoever the father is, there is more than enough of you to knock him off his perch. Your blood will be coursing through every inch of that child you are carrying. It will be just the two of you, an army of two, ready to do battle.'

I am willing strength on her but I am fearful at the thought of Maria being side-lined into the unyielding state of motherhood. That would be such a waste. Still, there is very little wrong in the world that cannot be softened by the sweet smell of a baby's skin. I immediately wished it would be a little girl, to let me imagine how my own daughter would have grown up.

'I've decided I do want to keep it. My mother said she will look after it and that I should get back to modelling as soon as possible afterwards. It will be fine. I would prefer a spring baby to a winter baby but I'm afraid that kind of timing is out of my hands.' She seems to have a sudden burst of energy.

'Come on, you can help me because today is moving day. We've a new place near the bottom of the hill. Mind you, this is only going to take about two or three runs for all the things we have accumulated over the past few years, so trust me, I won't be taking up too much of your time. My lifetime's belongings don't amount to much.'

We navigate our way back to Maria's little home in Montmartre in idle gossip, the way we have done so many times over the years, our chatter sealing us in a bubble of oblivion. A knife-wielding lunatic could jump in front of us and then plunge his knife into the neck of a passing child, and we would barely notice. We place several small bundles into a handcart with both of us then steering it down the hill until we reach the narrow Rue Poteau and Maria's new lodgings: a small apartment on what is a dark and dingy street. Maria and her mother have moved so often that she hardly comments on it at all anymore. She registers my disapproval.

'It will do for the moment. It is cheaper, and we don't have that much money coming in with even less for the foreseeable future.'

'If there's ever anything I can do to help you, Maria.'

'I know, but you have your own mother to worry about. You are going to have to make some decisions there.'

My mother has been suffering frequently with violent headaches, but sometimes I prefer them to her quiet moments where she appears to be nothing but an emptied hulk, her eyes devoid of light. Each time I sponge her at night, I study her frail body for lesions or swellings, terrified in case there is any evidence of the pox as there is a muted obsession with it around here. It is not something that is openly discussed, just darkly hinted at. Prostitutes are fearful of it and men are fearful of prostitutes giving it to them. But then if men like Manet can get syphilis, can they not just as easily pass it on? Did father's Marseilles trips harm *Maman* in any way?

One evening at the café, I listened as the men spoke gravely of a fellow artist who had just undergone treatment for syphilis. They described some sort of mercury stew where their friend had to sit in a small steam-room covered head to toe in mercury ointment while wrapped in blankets for twenty or thirty days at a time. Most of his teeth fell out and his jaw swelled painfully. The secretions from his nose and mouth had a disgusting smell, and he had fainted several times. They said he hadn't been right since and certainly didn't have the energy to do anything. To my shock, I heard them say that another friend had died of a heart attack during the treatment.

I have to be strong enough for both of us and I worry that I will find it too difficult. Agnes is the only one that knows, really. Agnes is a witness to something very different in me. She is like a beautiful mirror that I am drawn to yet don't want to stare at for too long. Agnes reveals to me a truth that I would much rather keep tucked away. We both know that something at the core of me is fragile and unpredictable, something has been dislodged, and I can only blame my grief for that. This has been playing a lot on my mind lately. I try to over-ride it by focusing on living in the moment, but there are incidents, fleeting events, where I feel in a daze, as if displaced.

And there is something that has been bothering me. One of those partly dreamt images, in those half-waking moments when the night is at its blackest. I see the Spaniard, crumpled in a heap at the bottom of the stairs, a small crimson pool seeping into the floorboards by his head. It seemed so real to me one night, that I fumbled in the dark to find something to mop up the blood. I awoke in the morning clutching a single, white glove.

SMOKY LEATHER

Philippe has promised to take me gambling. I have heard about this game called Roulette and it sounds fantastically reckless. I don't think it's legal, but Philippe has assured me that these gambling houses are very discreet. This seems to be the case when we arrive at a large house that is indistinguishable from the others along the street. A servant shows us up several flights of stairs to where a gracious woman in strings of pearls greets us warmly. Philippe shakes several of the gentlemen's hands and bows before a couple of the ladies, while I take in the scene. I wander over to the long table which is the focus of the room. The table surface is covered in a soft green cloth, and there is a wheel in the middle of it. A circle of red leather chairs have been placed around the table with most of them occupied. Philippe remains standing with a cigarette in his hand by a fireplace with some of the other gentlemen.

'Are you going to play?'

A young, thin man is at my side.

'I'm afraid I wouldn't have a clue.'

'It's quite simple. Do you like red or black?'

'I like the colour red. Black is so ominous.'

'Then red it is.' The young man places a coin on the red just before the man at the table's top shouts, 'No more bets.'

Everybody watches the wheel spin.

'Black loses. Red wins.'

'You see, there you go, nothing to it.' The young man pushes several francs towards me. 'Your first game. That's all yours, you won it.'

'But I couldn't.'

'Red or black? It's not often in life where you get to make a choice so starkly limited with potentially so handsome a pay-off. The only other choice is when to stop, and that is the one that has caused so many downfalls.' He nudges my attention towards an intense, haggard-faced man who is nervously twirling his moustache and looks as if he hasn't slept in days.

'His wife has taken his children away before he ruined them all, and yet he can't stop. His furniture is being sold off piece by piece. He is convinced with one lucky spin, his life will turn around.'

'Isn't that possible?'

'It's all about luck, but there's good luck and bad luck and they don't come in equal measures. I am Vincent by the way.'

'Bab– , Lily. Pleased to meet you.'

'Well, Lily, do you want to hang on to your money or give it another flutter?'

'Red is still calling me a little. I'm going to put it all on red, seeing as it hasn't cost me anything.'

I push my stack of coins onto the red.

'Place your bets. Your bets, gentlemen, please. That's it. No more bets. Thank you.'

The wheel seems to spin longer this time until eventually it clatters to a halt.

'Black loses. Red wins.'

I find myself jumping up and with an unrestrained yelp of delight. I give Vincent a quick hug. 'I've won!'

'Probably more than you thought, because you let it ride twice and red has just won again. You have to lift your money otherwise it will stay on the table all night.'

The pleasant young man helps me scoop up my winnings.

'By my reckoning, that looks to me to be over a thousand francs. Maybe two.'

I can't help but clap and give my new friend another embrace. And then my eyes fall on the moustache twirler at the other end of the table, and he looks in such a distressed state that I am tempted to go over and split my money with him. Some divine logic, however, tells me it would be upsetting the balance of nature. I am inclined to believe that I would be intervening in a way I'm not meant to and that Luck would have her revenge. Philippe joins me at the table, wedging himself firmly in the space between Vincent and me.

'I see you either have had a strong case of beginner's luck or you have a natural flair for this.'

I am flushed with excitement.

'That, Philippe, would be my first mistake, to believe I have a flair for it. I was just lucky tonight. But what fun!' I am glad, also, that the distressed husband and father with the well-twisted moustache is here on my first night of gambling just as a spectre of how things can go so badly wrong.

He speaks softly to me. 'Be careful of that man you were

talking to. He is like a demon when he has had too much to drink.'

Perhaps, but he seems a perfect gentleman to me.

* * *

I decide to go and buy lots of cashmere first thing in the morning. I want to buy that very extravagant hat for Catherine that I remember her admiring in a shop window to see if that will cheer her up. I am concerned about Catherine; her mood is very low these days. I would also like to pay off Madame Del because I have learned by now that none of those lovely dresses in my room are free, and that I have been running up an account. Catherine has to stay at Madame's because she cannot afford to pay off her bill. She confided that she felt responsible for me ending up at Madame's house, because she made it out to be all so wonderful when she was talking to Cécilia. Cécilia had always lived such a tough life with her spells in and out of prison, that Catherine knew her young cousin just wanted to hear stories of another way of life. Catherine embellished her lifestyle to the extent that Cécilia longed to live it too. But since she knew she wasn't blessed with the good looks and manners required, the next best thing was to encourage me, her prison friend, to consider it.

I softly rap on her Catherine's bedroom door and sit on her bed while she twists her hair into little curls. 'Catherine, if I can get enough money to pay off your account, would you be happier to find yourself a little apartment somewhere?'

To my surprise, she begins to cry.

'If I tell you something, will you promise to keep it yourself?'

I nod. I can at least try.

'You know my Léo, he came to collect me the first day

you arrived. Well, we are in love. His family doesn't approve, of course, and have cut him off. He has enlisted to try to save up some money, but I promised him I'd try to have a little place of our own ready for when he gets back.'

Well that is it. I immediately decide to forgo my shopping trip and instead pay off Catherine's account to Madame Del so she can be free to start up again. Another visit to the roulette table is necessary but I know that Philippe will indulge me.

* * *

Two nights later, I am again staring into the centre wheel in the grand house. This game of random spinning could help change Catherine's life.

'I shall be most cross if you start sprouting a moustache.'

I look up on hearing the familiar voice of my gambling guide, Vincent.

'Do you know Monsieur, that red doesn't win every time after all?'

He smiles and takes up a seat beside me. 'Yes, funny that. And just as well for the sake of the house. Are you doing miserably?'

'Not great. Now that you're here, I'll switch to black.'

'Your bets gentlemen; your bets. That's it. Thank you, no more bets.'

I watch, mesmerised.

'Red loses. Black wins!'

'Vincent, you are the devil. What dark powers must you possess? I shall let it ride again and again.' Three times, red loses and black wins.

'You have no idea what this money will mean. I could kiss you.'

'Please do, I promise I shan't object.'

'Philippe may have a problem with that, don't you think?' Philippe is again smoking by the fireplace but keeping a watchful eye.

* * *

This morning, a huge bouquet of three dozen red roses arrived with a card.

A dozen for each spin and to remind you that red is still prettier than black. V. X.

Over breakfast, Madame Del commented on the wonderful scent.

'Lily, you have to remember that to be a true courtesan you must be recognised as the mistress of only one man at a time. That is not to say that you must confine yourself completely to him, so long as you do not embarrass him. Discretion is the key to ensuring an income from several sources.'

'I understand Madame.'

I smile to myself. Truth be told, I'm not attracted to either Philippe or Vincent, but both men are good company in their own ways. While I sat on Philippe's lap the previous few nights in the small front room and he nuzzled my neck and traced the length of my back with his long bony fingers, he confessed he did not have the vigour to do anything else. He seemed content though to just be as close as possible to me, to breathe me in. I let him cup my breasts as if he were a fruit merchant weighing up some new and exotic fruit, fearful of bruising them.

My focus now is on finding Catherine a little apartment so that she and Léo can set up home together on his return. Léo is managing to send a little money Catherine's way, so between that and what Catherine has put aside herself, the little place that was recommended to them on Rue Saint-Georges seems to fit the bill. It is sparsely decorated but freshly wallpapered. Catherine has already planned to replace the curtains and has decided on how best to arrange her belongings.

'We'll go and pick up some small pieces of furniture on Saturday and have them delivered. Before you know it, you will be hosting grand *soirées* here.'

I am happy to be able to help my friend. There was nothing I could have done for Cécilia and I hope I am not betraying her memory by making the life of her much envied cousin a little easier.

* * *

The Café Anglais is boisterous tonight. Our rather large group has been eating and drinking for three hours, and are trying to outdo each other in song. I am glad to see that Catherine's mood has lifted as I always felt that all she needed was some more attention. A quiet young blond man with a beautiful singing voice watches my every move adoringly. I have already passed a few very pleasant evenings in his company, but by this stage, it is becoming almost irritating. I have decided, therefore, that it would be much better if he started falling in love with Catherine instead, just to lift her spirits. Knowing that Catherine is a very good dancer, I suggest that we all head off to the Bal Mabille.

'To the Bal Mabille!'

Philippe leads the charge on my suggestion of a change of venue. He has definitely become more energised this past month. I have long forgotten his rudeness on our first meeting and have thankfully discarded the awkward bustle that he had initially favoured. He has also resisted taking out any of the other girls from Madame's house. I, by extension, have accumulated a very nice selection of jewellery that Philippe has given me.

The Bal Mabile is luminous in its beautifully arranged gardens, all decorated with lighted glass balls and coloured garlands and lanterns looped across the trees. It is a wonderful spectacle. The small orchestra is set up in the centre of everything, its music wafting alongside the Champs-Élysées. The wind is softly blowing and feather-whips a healthy glow on to the cheeks of both the men and women. Almost immediately, the blond man has edged alongside me and is asking me to dance. At least that is what he appears to be doing, presuming, as he does, that I am able to fill in the pauses around his sheepish stuttering.

'I really don't know how, and I don't want to look ridiculous. But if you could ask Catherine, then I could watch you both and maybe learn a little.'

The blond man is completely thrown by a refusal which somehow ends up as a compliment. He agrees to ask Catherine instead, almost thanking me for the privilege of allowing him to do so, content in the knowledge that I would be watching. I saunter around the parameter of dancers.

'Are you just going to wander and watch?'

I don't recognise the voice, but as I turn towards him, there is something familiar in his look. Where have I seen him before? 'Will you dance with me?'

I know that I have just refused the blond man the same request but I feel more inclined to engage with this man.

'If you saw me hoofing about like an untrained horse, you would turn around and walk away right this instant while your dignity is still in tact.'

'I was always told I was good with horses.'

He is leading me toward the centre of the dancing platform before I can raise any vigorous objections. Oh no, and it's a polka, a complicated dance. I have no option but to throw myself into it with uncoordinated abandon, like a marionette whose puppeteer is drunk. I catch the disapproving glances of some of the women behind their fluttering fans, but to be honest, I couldn't care less. My dancing partner seems inspired to lose his finesse as well, perhaps so as not to show me up by contrast, which is quite chivalrous of him. Or else he too is a really bad dancer, which would be most unfortunate.

'She has the coordination of a kitten on ice.'

Yes, I could hear that, as clearly as if it had been whispered directly into my ear. My partner also managed to pick it up just as the dance came to an end.

'Well, a rosette for the horse and some warm milk for the kitten. It's a good job I'm not allergic to animals, otherwise I fear I shall be covered in a constant rash around you.'

'And has that become your plan, so quickly?'

'Without a doubt.'

I can see Philippe approaching in long strides towards us. His hand outstretched.

'George, how nice to see you. Are your parents well? Lily, George shares an apartment with my nephew Gaston.'

'Yes, thank you, they are both in good spirits. Father's arthritis has been nagging him a little, but apart from that …'

Philippe is taking me by the elbow and steering me towards a small group of his friends. He wishes this George well for the rest of the night.

He rocks a little on his toes and calls after me, 'Thank you for the dance and I love your bracelet. I'd like to sketch it some time.'

Of course. It suddenly comes to me where I have seen him before. He is the dark young man who leaned forward and caught my eye several times at *Lakmé*. He probably knew I would be unlikely to remember him without some hint He must have known I was with Philippe on the night, and clearly made no approaches because of it. Ooh he is a slippery devil!

Philippe still has me by the elbow as he directs me towards a chair by a quiet table. He sits down beside me.

'My dear, I have come to a conclusion. I cannot keep up with the parade of young men who keep turning up at Madame Del's in the hope of securing your company for even one night, not to talk about these random swains that I'm going to have to constantly rescue you from each time we go out. Of that, I have little control. However, I can at least cut off the chain of supply that leads to Madame Del's door. So I have decided to put you in an apartment, a very fine little place a few streets off the Champs-Élysées on the Rue de Chaillot.'

'That would be nice, Philippe. Thank you.'

And with that, my freedom from Madame Del's brothel has been bought.

* * *

I pack up my little Japanese-print bag along with my much larger trunks and find myself lingering at the small iron gate that I had first walked through all those months earlier. Madame Del gently crushes me in an embrace.

'Madame, I really have no idea where I would be now if I hadn't come here. I honestly believe I could be dead.'

'Shush now. Remember I've been there. I've seen many young girls like you and always tried to help, as many times as they needed. It can be a cruel world for an unaccompanied girl. Now, if you see me in the street, you know you can call me Delphine.'

With one final backward glance, I climb into a waiting carriage. I know it is an act drenched in vanity, but I make the cab travel the length of the Champs-Élysées and back, partly so I can get my bearings but mainly so that I can be seen. I drink in the wide boulevards, the beautifully dressed people strolling with parasols and tailored frock coats, the large shop windows with fabulous dresses and hats, and even the small shop that sells nothing but chocolates. It must surely be the greatest display of decadence in the entire world: a shop that sells nothing but chocolate. A place you go into solely for the sake of indulgence.

The door to my very own apartment is three floors up. As I unlock it I am instantly met with the scent of lilies as if an invisible perfumed carpet was rolled out to greet me. The fire has been lit and it throws a reddish glow over the abundance of textures, from the tapestry on the wall, to the rich Indian carpets scattered across the floors. Panels of pristine lace peep out from between the plump plum-coloured curtains. I carry my bag into the bedroom which has a four-poster bed draped in muslin with red velvet cushions scattered matching the red velvet covered chairs. There are four Hokusai prints on the wall with their crashing waves and blue and white mountains, and I am touched by Philippe's powers of observation as he had clearly noted my little print bag and assumed, incorrectly, that I must be taken with things Japanese.

Spicy Incense

'I've found her!'

I am sitting in the Brasserie Andler and George has barged through the door.

'With dogged determination I've become an unequivocal pest. In fact I could make a livelihood out of this. Do detectives make much money?' He has bounded towards me like a puppy and is sprawling on the chair opposite me.

'Do you mean Babette?' This is so exciting. I feel my eyebrows reaching more skyward than I would have thought physically possible. What primitive instinct is this inclination to raise your eyebrows when surprised or shocked? And then I do the thing that I know looks ridiculous in others when embodying the same reactions … my mouth gapes widely, and indelicately, open. I of course then cover it with first one, then two hands, as if I have stumbled across some horror. He folds himself into a deep bow.

'The very girl. She was taken to Saint Lazare Prison.'

'Well, we must go there.'

'Fleur, you cannot just turn up and demand to be let in.'

Is some petty bureaucrat to be the final gate-keeper? I slump in disappointment.

'Which is why a contact had given me the name of someone I can make enquiries of, if we get there before he leaves for the afternoon.'

I lean across the table and kiss George on the forehead. He grabs his bowler hat, jams it on his head and reaches for my hand as we run out the door and onto the street searching out a cab.

'Can you afford this?'

'Much as I love to play the tortured writer, I do get a healthy monthly stipend from my father. It is more to protect his reputation than to keep me from rolling around in the gutter. No matter.'

He whistles loudly for the attention of a driver. As we clatter along, my mind unreels a scenario where Babette and I meet up again. Well, no, that is incorrect; where we meet for the first time, complete with introductions. I am unsure what I shall say to her. I silently practice, but it is like throwing a pebble down a deep well: nothing resonates. We arrive at the prison entrance. I stare at the imposing front door and immediately want to back away. George must go in alone to meet his contact, so I cross to the other side of the cobbled road and begin to aimlessly twirl the postcard stand on the corner. There are dull images of the Eiffel Tower and an ink drawing of a happy *marchand de coco*. I would love if a *marchand de coco* would walk around the corner this second with his big cylinder strapped to his back and pour me a nice soothing drink. Maybe it would calm me slightly. What other visual delights can I distract myself with? There is every manner of plump-cheeked women holding ridiculously large blooms to their faces and one silly woman framing herself with a heart-shaped floral creation of roses and peonies, coyly smiling from the stand at any passing would-be suitor. I would suggest he run for his life if he did see such a maiden rounding the corner framing herself in such way. It would, I believe, appear a little desperate. George is emerging from a side exit. But what is that gesture? He seems to be shaking his head and shrugging his shoulders as he approaches me.

'She's not there.'

'What?'

'No, no, it's fine. She was released into the care of her sister.'

'So she is free? Oh, thank God.'

I suddenly feel the weight of responsibility lift from my shoulders. I relax into a brief hug with George. 'Your mission is complete. She is probably this very instant having a picnic with her family. Look how glorious this afternoon is. In fact, let's make up a basket and go down by the Seine. I feel like some *brie*.'

The afternoon yawns and stretches before us like a cat in front of a fire. For the first time, in a long time, I can banish all thoughts of the patchouli girl. It is like the satisfaction of having completed a particularly difficult puzzle and just as easy to walk away from. We pick up a little *brie* and *roquefort*, two bottles of wine, bread, some *pâté de fois gras* and slices of glazed ham, then find a nice spot and spread out our little feast. I give the impression that I am surveying the people near the river, when really I am stealing glances at him. His long limbs are stretched out as he supports himself with one elbow while sipping from his glass. He slides so easily into these moments that I am envious. Whenever I am gifted such a pause, my mind becomes cluttered and urgent with the very many things I should be using that moment to accomplish. I spread the soft cheese on to a heel of bread and hand it to him.

'George, didn't you start off wanting to be a painter? Was it really of no interest to you at all?'

'I think it was more the idea of it that I wanted. You know, people strolling about the *Salon* admiring my work, admiring me by extension. But, when I came to Paris and met actual painters and realised how very grim many of them were … oh, and how hungry, come to think of it. The thing is I really don't like to be hungry. If I was laden down with God-given talent, I may have thought differently. It might seem a radical idea for many here to comprehend, but I like to eat.' He tops up my glass. 'I have an idea, Fleur. Why don't you come to the country with me this weekend? I know of a charming inn where we can hire out a boat. And there are beautiful gardens and lovely tea rooms.'

I pull my knees towards me and clasp my arms around them as he continues.

'We can book into two rooms. I don't mean to presume for one second …'

'George, I'm sure there are some very fine ladies who would jump at the chance to stroll around a scented garden with you.' Why am I doing this? He keeps reaching out, trying to make a connection, and I thwart him at every point. I begin clearing up the debris of the picnic. 'I have too much to be doing without ambling off among the flower beds.'

I can detect a look of irritation and impatience from George as he helps me clear up, and that is perfectly understandable. My attempts at conversation are met with silence as we leave the riverside. When we politely part at the bottom of Montmartre, I remind myself that, overall, it has been a very good day. Babette is safe and I need never think of her again. I now have a space in my mind which will soon, no doubt, be flooded very quickly with something else.

* * *

And I soon decide what that is to be. The bell is sounded and another service pronounced. I arrange five plates of green beans, fried with tomatoes and seasoned frogs' legs on my large tray then bend my head to inhale the steaming plates. Did they need more garlic? Balancing five large glasses of beer, I carry the small feast to a noisy table and stand back, watching the customers mindlessly gorge their food without care or curiosity, drowning each morsel with gulps of warm beer. Walrus is reading a newspaper while sipping at a *digestif.* I have been feeling strangely bereft without Babette and her patchouli rattling around my brain. Glancing around, I slide into the seat opposite him.

'Teach me about food.'

'Mademoiselle, if you are serious, nothing would give me greater pleasure. This is a precious art form, and I shan't have it besmirched by some ingénue. This for me has taken years of study; do you appreciate that? Worshiping and sharing at the tables of the greatest and most prodigious gourmands who ever lived. Is serving up this fodder to the sundry and indiscriminate palates that happen through these doors not sufficient?'

'Not any more. I want to excel at something, to have command over something. Do you understand?' Lowering my voice I find myself twisting a glass in front of me. 'I'd like to be able to make a statement, you know, to be surprising.'

With his soft, pudgy hand, Walrus pats mine affectionately.

'Then, my dear, you have much to learn, and we will start tomorrow afternoon with the street vendors, and by the time we get to the best place in Paris for meringues, creations as light and imperceptible as the flutter of an angel's wing, you will astound even yourself.'

* * *

And so it begins: my indoctrination. Waiting at the appointed spot on Rue Montorguell, I watch as Walrus approaches with a surprisingly light-footed step. He does not stop to exchange banter. He just barks at me to keep up, so I fall in step behind him.

This is my new mission. Last night, after my foolish behaviour with George, I had a strong urge to see him again and to tell him of my fear that I had fatally severed something between us. So after putting mother to bed and despite the heavy rain, I grabbed a shawl and ran through the streets until I was at the building where George lived. Even though it was getting very late, I climbed the stairs to the third floor and knocked on the door. I could hear some shuffling inside and, after a few moments, George's friend Gaston cracked open the door and, on seeing me standing there dripping, immediately invited me in. I told him I was sorry but needed to have a word with George. That's when he began to rub his head sheepishly and to look around the room as if he was being asked to conjure George up from behind the curtains.

'I don't think he's in, let me see. No, George isn't here.'

I stepped back and dropped my head in embarrassment while he tried to apologise for George's absence, as if somehow it was his fault. The rain seemed heavier as I pulled the shawl over my head and ran home, trying to avoid the puddles on the road. Why wouldn't he be off with another woman? He is perfectly free to do what he wants and it was improper for me to be turning up at a man's rooms anyway.

Gaston must now have the wrong idea entirely. I tucked myself tight in beside *Maman* on the bed and longed for simpler times. Which is why today, it is so reassuring to be in the company of someone who takes such an unequivocal delight in what many view as simply a basic sustenance.

'Have you any idea how fortunate you are to be French when it comes to food? We have the sublime influences of all those masterful chefs who had been attached to the great houses of the *ancien régime* until they fell through the revolution. How blessed are we who were not born into heightened circumstances, that these chefs then needed other work and our restaurants will forever reap the benefits. Do not look to any other country for your gastronomic impressions. The English, for all their arrogance, are only good for scorching perfectly decent joints or boiling chickens. The Germans cannot do sauces, and without them your food is naked, your art unfinished. Now Mademoiselle, a woman at a fine table is a mixed blessing, for even the most beautiful of them will not distract your attention from the pleasures of a good meal. Around a dining table, their scented allure only reinstates itself once coffee is served. This is something every woman, even the most beautiful, needs to understand. She must not allow herself to become tiresome. Look, here you'll find some of the most reliable oyster vendors in the city but I want to start you off simply.'

He takes my elbow and steers me over to a large man in a striped apron and after speaking quickly to him turns back to me instructing me to close my eyes and open my mouth. The taste is a mixture of sharp and sweet with a quality that I can only compare to something melting.

'Quail pâté soaked in Malaga wine,' he informs me.

I flick my tongue over my lower lip. 'Mmmm, it's lovely.'

'Now, across to a soup shop run by a very cranky lady. I think all of her love and passion goes into the soups so by the time the customers turn up, she is spent. I wanted to take you to my favourite butcher near Boulevard Saint-Germain, but the place was nearly burned to the ground recently due to some mob incursion, a riot of sorts. The influence of the Communards still abounds. Just because they were given amnesty a few years ago, today I cannot shop for pork flesh. The world is upside down.'

'Monsieur, I do not mean to show any disrespect but why do you come into our little café on such regular a basis?'

Walrus stops and smiles.

'It's part of my daily constitutional. I need a slight break between meals and your café is a convenient halfway point for two of my regular restaurants. And the waitresses are most pleasant to look at. It all goes towards building up an appreciable appetite.'

We walk on a little and pause in front of a narrow shop with one small window. Walrus lifts the latch and steps down into the small steamy room, its aromas bringing me back to the kitchen of my childhood winters.

'Here we are. Now what you should know about soup is that it can be very underestimated and misunderstood, like the pretty little sister in the family who is overlooked by her more glamorous older sister. Because soup is so comforting, many mistake that it for something quite pedestrian, whereas it is really the great tease, a portent, the overture, and should be approached with love. Yes, a good soup heightens expectations and that is the desired state to be in while approaching any table.'

He pronounces that we are to go to Les Halles and into the belly of Paris where we will do some promiscuous inhaling around the stalls. And I have to say that I love this sensation of being buffeted from one stall to the next, engulfed in flavours and smells and sensations. As I follow in the wake of Walrus, I feel he could navigate the market blindfolded, led simply by his nose. He brusquely name-checks the salt cod, carp, mackerel, herring, turbot and sturgeon at the fish stall, as if he were a general ordering them to fall into line. His voice lowers slightly and lilts with a nostalgia one normally reserves for absent friends as he discusses the merits of the various vegetables, for most are out of season. He outlines the peculiarities of cabbages, onions, artichokes, asparagus, showing special reverence for celery which he claims gravely and respectfully, is an aphrodisiac that should be eaten only sparingly by bachelors.

He plunges my hands into a mound of pistachio nuts and then his own, sinking and luxuriating in what he describes as a perfumed wonder to be savoured delicately on the tongue. I am tingling with the assault on my senses and the crispness of the Parisian air. And the spices … everything about spices is exotic: Turmeric, Garam Masala, Cinnamon, Mustard Seeds, Saffron. It makes me think of Marco Polo and grand adventurers stumbling across these wondrous mystical powders.

Through my incense haze, I manage to identify a passing George, between the potatoes and tomatoes. Walrus immediately raises his eyes skyward.

'This, Mademoiselle, is why women will only ever be good at *cuisine de la ménage*. Domestic cooking is women's work, because they are far too easily distracted to be great in the kitchen. Only men have the dedication and temperament to elevate it to an art. Go, go! Your young man may blink and miss you.'

I shout out George's name to get his attention as he seems deep in thought. Or maybe he is ignoring me. But on the second try he turns, and I am relieved to see he is smiling. I weave over to him.

'I thought I saw you there.' I feel sure that Gaston would not have mentioned my surprise visit last night, but then what do I know about the pact between men.

'Fleur, how nice to see you.' We walk on a little in silence.

'How is your writing coming along?'

'I was beginning to lose patience with it. My idea was to chronicle day-to-day lives in the form of a diary. I thought it would be – I'm not sure exactly – a more elevating experience; you know, amusing. But I have upturned a lot of self-inflicted degradation, a dedicated pursuit of scrounging as a compass for living and a whole world of mediocre talent. This Montmartre life is all slightly unhinged and sordid. I'm not sure if I have the patience or curiosity to pursue it to any great degree.'

'So you have briefly feasted on Montmartre and now you have indigestion?' I have instinctively decided to employ the culinary allusions that so readily trip off Walrus's tongue.

'You see I've been trying to gather witticisms, repartee, anecdotes, and all I seem to be recording are meaningless theories and joyless jokes.'

'George, you are just a literary odd-job man at the moment and these traits you're trying to find, well, people use them as a bartering tool and as a trade-off. They will bring them the table, if you provide the table. I see it every day at work; if somebody tells an amusing tale or sings a bawdy song, they will have a drink bought for them or a plate of food put before them.'

George smirks a little. 'Do you believe it is all right to be unscrupulous in the pursuit of your art?'

'Well I believe that great artists and writers, if they are committed, have an imperative to follow through on what is inside them. They probably have no choice in the matter. *Mon Dieu*, you are grim and distracted.'

'Would you forgive anything if it led to a great work?'

I fear I would forgive him anything – but say nothing. He shrugs his shoulders. It's best to part from his company rather than being brought down by his mood.

* * *

Back in *patron*'s kitchen, I continue to surreptitiously tip cognac into the soup. He has wondered aloud at the upturn in its popularity. When he cooks mackerel, I add about half a glass of Champagne and some olive oil to the stock. That dish too, quickly becomes a favoured request, so much so that he has to increase his order for mackerel. I have much to be grateful for in the convivial and unmeasured approach with which drink is served at the café.

But at night under my covers, with the reassuring sound of *Maman*'s laboured breathing rattling through the stillness, it creeps over me like small insects scrambling from my toes to my hairline. It is a sense of unease. I am caught in what seems to be somebody else's dream, trapped inside a big clear balloon, bouncing along until the lion's head of the studio door winks and admits me. This time I look closer. He is face down; his dark curls blood-caked. No one else is around. His long, paint-stained fingers are splayed as though to allow one to trace around each one individually, as a child does its own hand. I step over his left boot, which is crooked at an awkward angle and then outside into the rain. And it rains and rains and when I lift my head, my hair is a cloying web encasing my face and Isobel is still blanketed in the gritty sodden earth.

Damp Lavender

There are times when I forget the reality of my circumstances – like yesterday, when Catherine and I strolled in and out of shops ordering pieces of furniture for her little apartment along with new hats and capes and cashmere wraps. We found some soft butterscotch leather gloves and I insisted on buying four pairs, two pairs each for when the weather becomes cooler. I seem to have the need to buy things, as if I am trying to build a fort around myself. I have convinced myself that people will be distracted by my things, by my finery, and not look any closer.

But then my reality betrays me, as it did when Vincent turned up at Madame Del's house before I left, and asked for me. Unlike Philippe's tentative explorations, Vincent put a value on his franc. He had been drinking, but we both knew he was entitled to lay his greasy head on my naked stomach, to plunge first his fingers then his cock into me as he roared his exclamations so loudly that I'm sure even Hélène down in the kitchen could hear. To then lap up the sweat sparkles from my skin with a surprisingly soft tongue and when the taste of me roused him yet again, to enter and pump me, workmanlike, each pump eliciting a more ecstatic prayer to the Lord above while I merely wondered how Hélène could have missed so obvious a cobweb in the corner of the ceiling.

Yesterday afternoon, I sat thinking about this as I drank some lemonade on my balcony watching the streets below. I cast my eyes across the many, many rooftops, knowing that the closer they huddled towards Montmartre, the less grand they would become. I like the fortitude of these fine strong buildings as they demand to be noticed along the leafy boulevards, unlike those in the poorer areas that seem to apologise for their existence, each one haphazardly insinuating itself on to the next in the manner of drunkards weaving their way home.

I thought of those early days; of the smell of paint thinner and dusty floorboards; of rough crimson-stained fingers as they tore at my clothes, of crushing loneliness and gnawing fear. And I thought of Madame Delphine who advised me to make my trades wisely.

* * *

So here at the Café Anglais, with the blond Baron playing some tunes on the piano, while Catherine watches him with a growing affection, I can quite easily relegate the fact that Vincent seems to have fallen in with our company, claiming some loose alliance with Philippe through their attendance at various functions. Philippe is regaling the table with stories of his time as a doctor in the court of Napoleon III as Vincent slides further into inebriated unpleasantness, clearly looking for a quarrel. Unwittingly, I give him the opportunity when he catches sight of my evidently rapturous expression as George enters the restaurant and joins our table. His friend and Philippe's nephew, Gaston, follows along behind him. Philippe gestures towards the waiter.

'Two more settings, but first two more glasses.'

George whispers close to my ear as he passes behind my chair.

'In my experience, pretty girls travel in pairs so I brought Gaston along just in case.'

He takes his place further along the table. With studied precision, Philippe tops up each person's glass from a newly opened bottle of Champagne. I am aware of Vincent redistributing his light frame in his chair, a scowl darkening his face. I feel trapped.

'Could you please slip more into Mlle Lily's glass?' He slurs in a menacing tone. 'It seems the only chance I'll have with her is if her senses are deadened.'

Vincent is oblivious to the fiery look that George shoots in his direction. My glance flits immediately to George and I have not even registered Philippe.

'Seriously though, Mademoiselle,' I feel hot pinpricks spreading across my chest as Vincent pushes his chair slightly back from the top of the table and slowly crosses his legs, 'Is it patience that I need more of? Is it Champagne that you need more of? Could it be money?' He fumbles for his pocket.

This is it. I am being humiliated and there is little I can do about it.

George jumps to his feet and, with one hand, grabs Vincent by his throat, his chair momentarily tilting back on two legs. Gaston and the Baron immediately spring to pull George away and the chair rocks and rights itself again leaving Vincent coughing and rubbing his neck. Undeterred, George points his finger close to Vincent's face.

'You show a bit more respect in the company of ladies or I'll throw you out of here myself. Go sup with the devil and learn to keep away from decent company.'

Vincent gives a large whoop and a clap.

'Decent company? Decent company? My dear boy; that has made my night. Ask the doctor there, what price decent company comes by these days in Paris.'

And there it is. I have been unveiled with the flourish of a freshly planed sculpture at the Exhibition. He has yanked the cloth from me and presented me, stone cold, to an assembled audience for inspection and comment. And I can only sit here, petrified. I am aware that Catherine is draping my wrap around my shoulders.

'Come, let's leave.'

My palms are cold and tingling and Catherine gently nudges me again. Vincent has a contorted smile from having achieved − I am not exactly sure what. He is a loathsome specimen and he has rendered me immobile. Babette, you have made your choices, and you had reason to make those choices. You promised yourself you would live by them. Do not sit here as if you are some pathetic foil of destiny − it has been yours to shape. My resolve has returned. I straighten my back and rise from my seat, passing wordlessly to the other side of Vincent's chair. I slowly pick up a jug of iced water and empty it on to his lap.

'There isn't enough Champagne or money in this entire world, Vincent,' I lean in closer to whisper, 'and the pity for you is that you know what you'll be missing.'

* * *

It is morning, and I have received flowers from Philippe, flowers from George and a note from Vincent to say he is leaving for Australia. Fortunately, I have a day with Catherine planned and I accompany her to the platform at Gare de l'Est as she waves the Baron off on the Orient Express. His own father arranged for him to see a doctor in Vienna, believing his health to be far from robust. Catherine is seeing him off on a long break to take some invigorating spring waters somewhere, and she is at the same time torn, not knowing where her beloved Léo is nor in what condition. I think she is replacing her anxiety by fussing over the Baron.

It is why, I believe, so many women lavish such affection on their cats or their horses. It is all a displacement for real love and tenderness. All that nuzzling into warm animal flesh, when really, if they would only admit to it, they would much rather be writhing under a naked man who adores them. I have seen women acknowledge their husbands with only a cursory nod as he enters a room, then in pads a cat and her eyes will light up and she will immediately call it to her lap and speak in intimate soothing tones into its velvet ears. I blame the husband. He does not see that instead of his perfunctory response to his wife before he proceeds to the fireplace and lights up a pipe, he should make his way over to her chair, lift her face lovingly and kiss her deeply. The cat would soon be banished.

Catherine staggers slightly as the blue and gold sleeping cars of the train pull away and I lead her to a bench.

'You look pale.' When I think about it, this has crossed my mind before.

She smiles weakly. I have just this second come up with a very good idea.

'Catherine, why don't you move in with me? You would be saving money. Then closer to the time that Léo is expected back, we can look for a nice little place for you both. In the meantime, you won't be wasting what little resources you have.'

''Babette, you are presuming a lot of Philippe, and George might resent having to navigate around me every time he comes to call.'

'Nonsense. I think they would both be pleased that I have a companion. Philippe has said the apartment is mine to do with as I wish, and he would hardly begrudge me having my dear friend move in.'

'Babette Fournière, you would have people doubt the wetness of water if you put your mind to it. Fine, fine. I haven't the energy to argue with you.'

I can be such a clever thing sometimes!

'This will be so amusing. Let's go fill a trunk with your belongings.'

Neither of us have any idea when Léo would be able to come home or how long this arrangement is going to last but hopefully there will be at least a few months of girls' outings and trips to the shops and long wine-soaked lunches, more energetic evenings at the Bal Mabile and lots of fending off of potential suitors together. Catherine is a firm friend, closer than any sister could be.

* * *

My friend, my sister, is fading. Philippe has ordered her to the hospital. She has been lacking energy and her pallor was becoming more alarming by the day. It confused me because her eyes were shining and her skin had a flushed quality, both of which I foolishly mistook for being hallmarks of a young woman in love. It was her cough, a belligerent hacking that had burrowed deep into her chest, which made me finally call for Philippe. A childish belief in magical thinking made me delay it for longer than was beneficial to Catherine. Her weight loss was instantly apparent to him. I, however, was oblivious to it and teased her for her lethargy.

And now I am holding back her hair as she tries to retch into a basin by the side of her hospice bed, tuberculosis rattling her tiny frame. My skirts trail these long corridors day after day as I refill jugs of water to keep her thirst quenched and her forehead cooled. Philippe is angry with me, telling me to allow people whose job it is to take care of Catherine. I read to her, sometimes passages from the Bible. I felt, if I didn't, I would be divinely rapped on the knuckles. I felt that I needed to barter with God so He would speed up Catherine's recovery. Mostly I read from popular Gothic novels to keep her mind active and emotions engaged.

The coughing that surrounds me is like a rolling death rumble. It starts in the far bed in one corner and reverberates. It inhabits the night-gown-draped patients so completely and ferociously that it sometimes bends them in half as they struggle to expel it, to exorcise it from deep within their being. They then collapse back down, spent from the effort, until the low rattle begins deep within their chests again. It is a pitiful duel. Catherine is so weak. Where will her strength come from when she is next seized by this beast lurking within her? I want to prod her so that she will be energised and prepared. I want her to raise her puny fists and excoriate this fiendish intruder.

But she is slipping. In her fevered confusion, she is convinced that I am her young cousin Cécilia.

'Ceci, I am so sorry for being so unkind to you.'

I take her hand and hold it to my face, kissing it softly.

'Ceci, I am so sorry …'

'Catherine, I have always loved you and admired you, and always thought you beautiful.'

'Thank you, Ceci, you're a good girl …'

Catherine smiles and I squeeze her clammy hand. Her face is serene. One deep unbroken breath emanates from within her, her chest rising with the effort. Her eyes flicker closed and then her breath rattles in an extended surrender.

'Catherine. Catherine?'

I feel detached. I have never before seen life ebb so distinctly away, from the shallow breaths to this nothingness, this abject stillness. The careful way that she pinned her hair, the rose water she dabbed on her skin and clothes, the powder she used on her face, the graceful way she swept her hands through the air while telling a story: all the details that made up Catherine as a person are suddenly extinguished. Her essence is gone, like the smothering of a flame, despite her living image lying stilled on the bed before me. It is a cruel taunt, this death.

George is waiting for me on the street outside my apartment. I lean into him as I traipse heavily up the stairs. I feel exhausted, emptied. I go straight into my room and ease myself on the bed. He lies down beside me and I am aware of him rocking me as I cry myself into a dulled exhaustion.

* * *

The maid is not the brightest and often needs more instruction than I have the patience to give her, so it is pleasant to see the table freshly laid with hot rolls, coffee, juices and fruits, and several cuts of *charcuterie* by the time I get up. I haven't breakfasted like this in a very long time. I feel she must be responding to the male presence in the household and is in search of a type of validation that clearly I am unable to give her. Or perhaps George has simply told her what to do and what to purchase. I do not want to draw too much attention to the novelty of this morning's feast in case he thinks I am unable to handle the help properly. The maid, who has some Biblical name like Marie or Marthe, is scurrying about with unseemly purpose, clearly in an attempt to give the impression to George that this sort of domestic busyness is the norm for her. So we both pretend, for the sake of appearance and both our reputations, that today is unfolding no differently to any other day. George reads the newspaper and sips at his coffee, oblivious, while the maid and I daren't look directly at each other, neither of us wishing to make a dent in George's silent approval of the day so far.

George's upbeat mood yanks me a little from the experience of having watched Catherine die. In fact, he always lifts me. I intended to wallow in misery and to shroud myself in mourning for at least a week, but already I am feeling a little flighty. Poor Catherine. I will miss her. But how does George manage to smell of freshly picked lavender? Does he keep a small bottle of cologne on his person? His hair is a little dampened from the wash bowl and has sprung into untamed ringlets. He will later rake through it with something greasy from a little pot, the same way my father used to, and it will take on a smooth sheen. But I like this look, maybe because it speaks of a certain intimacy, casual and untamed and lacking the patina that he presents to others.

He rattles his cup back down on to his saucer, and with a quick snap he folds the newspaper and tucks it under his arm in one fluid movement.

'Mar— will you tidy up my bed now, please.'

She obliges immediately. She could have at least finished drying the plate that was in her hand. When I say 'now', I don't mean it as literally as she understands it to be. I really must learn to instruct her more sequentially and not presume she will make independent judgments, for all that does is force me to begin my day on an empty stomach.

'George,' I brace myself. 'You really are owed an explanation.'

I could not bear to be in a constant state of worry about meeting another Vincent out in company in similarly excruciating circumstances.

'You've been so good and so sweet to me, that there's something I have to tell you. Philippe is not just the generous benefactor that I may have led you to believe him to be.'

'My darling Lily, I have long known about Madame Delphine's house. I can honestly say to you that I do not care. I could wring your neck for the way you make me feel about you and then wring everybody else's if they so much as glance in your direction. It's a predicament with which I am completely unfamiliar. Could we not make this little apartment your sole orbit? Do you really have to venture out in society at all?'

'You can imagine how that would cease to be amusing for me within a very short space of time. You want me trapped, bored and gagged? I'd be clawing your eyes out very quickly and you'd regret the day you first saw me.'

'Right, for my own self preservation, I shall return and take you out to dinner later. We'll raise a glass to Catherine. Will you be fine for that Lily?'

'And George, I'm not …'

But he makes his way towards the door, the newspaper still carefully tucked beneath his arm.

'I think you need some more rest. You have had a tough few weeks and I could do with some fresh air.'

And there it is, with a wink and a meltingly warm smile, as if under a cloudburst of petals, the air seems to have sweetened and I can breathe more easily. He loves me too.

STALE TURPENTINE

With my hands clasped around this small glass of beer, I stare into it as if it is a pool of wisdom. I stare until the rim of froth dissolves. What answers do people seek at the bottom of these glasses? What spell of introspection does this contrary liquid cast on them? It mesmerises, hour after hour, night after night. Downcast eyes hypnotised by the amber brew, seeking redemption or temporary ease from a cluttered mind. I can only conjure up images of a half-dead mother, or at least that is what she exudes. Her sadness is a resting beast that she is afraid to stir, so she remains still. Still and wearied by the effort.

I find myself talking in whispers in case the beast consumes us both. And in those moments, my baby whimpers for attention. My Isobel and all thoughts of her must be swaddled until she is nothing but a hollow stirring. I would otherwise rise up in a rage and rouse the beast and we would all be lost.

I have not been sure that I can entrust this to George and I am even less sure now as I wait for him, than when I contacted him. I watch for his bobbing hat among all the others crisscrossing these narrow streets. I glimpse him, striding effortlessly up the hill.

The images of the cracked head of the dying painter and the blood-soaked floorboards rise up like night-time intruders, making me sit bolt upright to banish them to the moon-shimmered Montmartre rooftops. But they are returning with more frequency.

'My dear Fleur, you look lovely sitting here in the late morning sun.' He swivels to catch the eye of a waiter and calls for a Kirsch.

I lean forward, both arms resting on the table in front of me. 'George, there is something still troubling me about the death of the Spanish painter.'

George accidentally nudges his paper on to the floor and bends to pick it up. He smooths it out and places it first to his right, then to his left. He has now pulled his chair too close to the table so scrapes it back a little to allow enough room to cross his legs. I wait for his fidgeting to stop.

'The painter? Are you still concerned with that? Did you not invest more than enough of your time on that whole business chasing after the model girl and all that? He's dead. What more is to be said?'

'I think … there's something … in my mind. Something tells me I was there.'

He plants both feet firmly on the floor and leans towards me.

'I have this strong sense that I was there. I can see him. I even think there is a faint breath still in him. But I do nothing.'

This is so hard to tease out in my head, which is why I must say it out loud to try to make sense of it. My lost moments usually only throw up some indiscretion like ending up entangled in the arms of a strange man and wondering how I met him, but the Spaniard's hallway is giving me that same aftertaste where my mind becomes like a jumbled ball of wool that I must patiently unravel.

'It is all so vivid. I'm standing looking down at him. The air is stifling … there is a smell of a mixture of turpentine, and sweat, and, and … I'm not sure what else. His head is at an angle and he is wedged against the front door.'

'Fleur, these are just bad dreams. He was found at his easel.'

'No. No. You see that was the rumour going around and that is the first time I knew for sure that something wasn't quite right, because I knew he was at the foot of the stairs and not in his studio. George, I think I may have had something to do with it. I may have killed him.'

There! I've said it out loud. There is a lingering pause, and then George laughs, casting his eyes towards the ceiling.

'You killed him? And why in God's name would you have done that and what makes you think that you could. Fleur, you're starting to worry me. This is ridiculous. Let's have another drink.'

And this is where I must decide: do I unburden myself to George and alert him to my fragile mental state, to the moments of anxiety that are so crippling that can render me immobile? I bite down on my lip as George sips at his drink. I really do want to pledge myself to him here and now, whatever he wishes that to mean. The few times, more frequently than I would care to admit, that I had allowed my imagination to wander down the rose-scattered path of romance, I would try to stop myself, vowing that I would not become exposed to the certain heartbreak I would suffer when he would up and leave, as I knew he would. But then I would hear Maria in my head telling me I should just live in the moment. Maybe if I got myself a job somewhere like a luxury goods shop, maybe working in an environment like that would make me seem more respectable to George or to his family.

I had never really considered it before, although mother always said that pretty girls of poor means could only chance upon a rich husband by working in a decent shop, somewhere the gentlemen would come to buy expensive gifts. Trying to so manipulatively land a rich husband had just never occurred to me before. But to fall in love with someone who happened to be wealthy – that, by my own code, was less unseemly. I spread my palm out on the cool marble top so that my finger tips grazed George's. He immediately pulls his hand away and gulps down the last of his beer. In that second, I realise I have lost him.

* * *

Things are made clearer, though no less burdensome, in the letter I receive from George. It reads as follows:

My dearest Fleur,

You are too good a friend to me to be treated as cowardly as this. However, it is out of fear of losing your friendship that I have chosen to contact you in this way. You see, I have fallen deeply in love with a young lady and it is tearing me apart. What started off as a casual acquaintance slowly grew until it has completely and feverishly consumed me.

I always thought warmly of you. I hope, after some deliberation, you would see fit to keep me in your life, but I would understand if you chose instead to release me to the wind like a discarded feather. I would miss your friendship, your company, your complicated intelligence, so think kindly of me as you ponder your decision.

Yours,

George

The café is a sanctuary where I can easily become distracted by the transformational powers of a sprinkling of tarragon, but at home, *Maman* now needs my entire concentration. Last night, I couldn't stop myself from staring at her arms as I sponged them with warm soapy water. These arms, with skin now like crêpe, once used to hug me and protect her. Arms against which I could brace myself from whatever onslaughts a little girl could conjure up: scary monsters under the bed, the moon falling from the sky, baby birds being blown out of their nests because the wind was too strong, and the greatest fear of all, that of losing her. These pale, skinny arms were once my shield. The fingertips were salty against my lips as I kissed them gently.

I could try, but I know that I'm unable to wash away the cloying layer of sadness and confusion that thickens on her pale skin just that little more each day. Nor can I sponge away the rash on her palms and soles of her feet. I have so far ignored it, but I fear that this may be a sign of syphilis that seems to be stalking certain areas and households. I fear that only a short-term hospital spell will give her the best chance, not arsenic, or blood-letting, not fresh air or the daily bottle of claret in a Bordeaux blend, all of which had been recommended as cures. I am not protecting her by trying to convince myself that warm tubs of lavender infused water will make all the difference. I cheered us both up by frying up some herring with mushrooms, shallots and a bunch of chervil which we ate in contented silence.

* * *

We are taking another trip out to the Bois de Bologne and the circus. Maria, who has been sketching away her boredom and confinement as she is due within a matter of weeks, has talked me into it.

'There must be some way of speeding up this process.'

I suppose it is not unreasonable to believe that the grind and crunch of a train on a track would go some way towards jolting a new life from even the snuggest of wombs. Maria rubs her swollen stomach and looks pleadingly at me, as if there were something – anything – I could do.

'Very soon you might be ruing the day you were in such a rush to get that baby out. At least now you have a bit of control over your time. That will be gone as soon as the little Emperor or Empress makes an appearance. It could be a holy terror when it arrives.'

'I'm terrified Fleur.'

'It will be fine. Yes, painful but you just have to remind yourself that it won't last forever. When Isobel was born, if you had handed me fifty thousand francs, I wouldn't have been able to recall the pain with any great accuracy.'

'It's really not the pain that I'm terrified of.' Maria rubs her belly. 'It's what will become of me. What about my life? My choices? Fleur I can't tell you how much resentment I've felt over this little creature. I've already cast it in the role of some scowling Mother Superior who is out to do nothing but restrict me. My lovers? My modelling? My painting? I have this crushing feeling that my life is over.'

In my heart of hearts, I cannot reassure her that her

mother will be there to help her because Madame Valadon is nothing but a gnarled, gin-soaked crow, who seems to lack any warmth. In fact, I fear for the child's wellbeing, unless Maria takes complete charge, which clearly is not an idea that she relishes. One of them is going to have to work, and as a charwoman, I am not sure how much in demand Madame Valadon continues to be. She undoubtedly was hard-working in her day, and had even scrubbed the floors of the Café Guerbois, but the flask welded to her hip seems to demand most of her attention most of the time.

But sometimes, there has been a glimmer of something else. A number of days ago, when I was visiting Maria who was clearly in great discomfort, I turned at the sound of a heavy-footed approach and with the howl of an outside gale at her back, Maria's mother heaved open the door and shook a powdering of early snow from her shoulders. She peeled away her shawl and draped it over a chair. She jerked her head at me and motioned me towards the door, signalling me to get out and leave them alone now that she had returned. Madame Valadon took a quick sip from her flask, wiped her nose with her sleeve and pulled up a small stool beside her daughter. I hated having to leave and glanced back with fury at the old lady, but saw that she was holding Maria's hands in her own and covering them with soft kisses. I watched as mother and daughter locked eyes and what I realised I was witnessing, was tenderness.

Maria is suddenly surging with energy now that we have arrived at the circus – even more so upon her uncle's approach. He seems to have been expecting her. I suddenly feel at a loss as they whisper conspiratorially.

'Uncle has set something up for you, Fleur.'

I am led over to a practice ring where trapeze artists normally run through their routines. Uncle unravels a swing and lowers it closer to the dirt ground. He stands behind it, tightly clasping the roughly hewn ropes with his wide hands.

'Fleur, this was always my thinking place. I would sit here and swing higher and higher until my thoughts were flung upwards and out into the clear, blue sky.'

I am confused and a little embarrassed. I would have presumed that my demeanour was always one of cool indifference that betrayed nothing of my inner turmoil. I batten down my anxieties everyday and project instead an exaggerated concern for every misfortunate soul who trundles across my path. I am a fraud and a shameless abuser of other people's vulnerabilities because I am so full of fear. Maria is my oldest friend, so how presumptuous of me to think that I can fool her. I obediently position myself on the slim bar and rock a little on my rump to tug my skirts out from under me so they are not in a bunch. Uncle speaks in a voice that has the weave of a vagabond life, all knotted and sinewy, firm, strong and sure, as compacted and steady as the rope that is rutting into my hands.

'Hold on tight', he instructs close to my ear, with the low growl of an earth rumble, 'and let go.'

And I know what he means, the minute I gulp in that first patch of sky blue. 'Let go.' Not of the rope but of the weightiness that grounds me, that has me shuffling and dead-footing any lightness of being I once possessed.

Swing.

The surge of air tugs and loosens my hair.

Swing.

My cheeks feel as if they are being lightly slapped.

Swing.

I fling my head further back, trusting the sky won't drop me to the earth.

Swing.

My eyes snap tightly shut. And I see …

Swing.

The body. The blood trickle. The shape of a woman.

Swing.

Am I looking up the stairs – or down the stairs?

Swing.

I am looking up. She's at the top of the stairs.

Swing. Whoooosh. Whooosh. Whoosh. Shush. Shhh.

* * *

Maria's baby, a boy she named Maurice, was born on the 26 December, at the tail end of the year 1883. I imagine that December babies are angry babies who grow into anxious people, because everything is in a headlong rush towards new beginnings. If it was a bad year, then people are happy to get it over with. If it was a memorable year, then there is a nostalgia and a desire to hold on to it. December comes round year after year, bringing with it a sense of closure, another year ended, another milestone against which you must measure accomplishments, aspirations and disappointments. December is a month to look beyond, because in January resolutions and hopes are invigorated and people dare to dream again. And to have the misfortune to be born so close to Christmas! I cannot imagine how that would frame your mindset. Your special day is tagged on as an extra nuisance to be served up with the Christmas left-overs. Me, I was born at the end of January, which has an oddly delusional bearing on me. I can always convince myself that this year will be different.

What can I say about Christmas? I brought my mother for a long walk. The snow has a way of blanketing even the most blackened cobbles in sparkles. Like crunching diamonds underfoot, you blink against the shattering brightness while the crispness of the air pin-pricks your face.

But since then, there has been a deep wound inside me, as if I have been clawed by some sort of trapped wild animal at the core of my being, severing my organs, my heart, with its sharp nails and teeth. A sense of rupturing making me feel as if I could bleed to death. She has been sent away. I couldn't bear to watch as, I'm sure, she pressed her face against the grill of the partially blocked window of the hospital car meekly, seeking me out. I wouldn't have been able to pretend. I remember when I was taken by the hand of a governess for the first time, and wondering as I turned to look pleadingly at my mother, why she was standing there calmly waving. I recognise now the pretence that was masking her face.

The doctor's advice was that she would be better monitored at the Petites Maisons Hospital, and I loudly reassured us both, as I packed her favourite nightgown, that soon she would be much stronger and that we would go on long picnics after I had collected her.

Without that small bit of extra income that my mother's needlework brought in, I very quickly realised that I would have to find a cheaper place to rent. I managed to do so a couple of streets away. One room, where a family of four used to live. What did I need really: a bed, a chamber pot and somewhere to light a fire.

'You will find redemption in a meringue.'

I have been absentmindedly wiping down the bar counter in wide heavy circles, and clearly Walrus has had enough. He is leaning out from where he is tucked into his panelled booth, as though his head has been disembodied in a magic trick.

'For all your knowledge, you really are a simple man. Aren't you?'

'I am a man of simple faith you could say. My stomach is my deity and I am a worthy and prodigious worshiper. Are you nearly complete here?'

'Another fifteen minutes or so. Why?'

'We shall go seek redemption. My sojourn here has been sullied by your less than convivial visage.'

And it's true; my mind is swamped with dark thoughts of my mother's incarceration and the horrors that she must be enduring and this shows in my face. The Petites Maisons Hospital, is not the place of rest and recuperation that a disengaged and disinterested doctor led me to believe, but a hell on earth where women are warehoused like shanks of meat piled upon one another and where sick women mingle with women who are completely insane. This has been gleefully narrated to me by busybodies, whose metier is gossip, dripping in horror and mortification. They get a kind of ghoulish pleasure in the misfortune of others. No, more than that, it is their life blood and they suck deeply for sustenance. It will poison them one day.

So I shuffle through the slush alongside Walrus until we come to a rough stone building on Rue de Richelieu. Walrus presents it to me with one long sweep of his arm, as if it exists through his sheer cleverness. He proclaims it, 'the finest *pâtisserie* in all the city' and hurries me inside. I am nudged toward a small table as he orders meringues and other delicacies. We wait in reverential silence until several plates are brought from the kitchen and fanned out before us: sorbets, ices, fruit, chocolate sauce and gloriously peaked fluffy white meringues. Walrus scoops something from each plate and I follow suit. With the very first spoonful, I close my eyes and smile, which a contented exhale warms my chest.

'Incomparably light, wouldn't you agree?'

I nod. Three careful spoonfuls later, I sit back a little in my chair.

'It's my mother. I thought I was sending her for treatment and what I have done is imprison her.'

Walrus raises one finger to his lips to quieten me.

'Mademoiselle, you are here to take pleasure not to seek consolation. To honour the art, you must banish your troubles and simply languish. Here, have some more meringue.'

He pushes my plate closer towards me and my fork crumbles through the delicacy like a padded foot on the softest of snowfalls.

Floral Citrus

'What's wrong. Tell me.'

I hate George to see me all puffy eyed and streaming and snivelly nosed, but he must be told.

'I've just heard from Philippe that the Baron is dead.'

George visibly relaxes as if he has just suddenly found his lost gloves or something of equal nuisance value.

'Yes, I suppose, well, he was a young man. So that is a pity.'

My blotchy face must be distracting as he is not deducing the horror of what I am revealing.

'No, you don't understand. He died of tuberculosis. It's my fault that Catherine is dead. He had been ill all along and I forced them together and then she got sick too and now she's dead.' I am suddenly seized by a compulsion to grab my throat and then feel my forehead with the back of first one hand, then the other. It is just dawning on me. 'This means, I could become ill too. What are the first signs of tuberculosis, George?' Why is he looking at me like that? And is that a smirk beginning to curl his lips?

'Marry me.'

'What?'

'Marry me, Lily. I need to protect you from yourself. I also need to do something to preserve my strength, otherwise I'd be dashing from one end of the city to the other monitoring every little sniffle and cough.'

'Are you teasing me George?'

'I want you to be my wife, but only if you don't get tuberculosis. I'd hate to have to drag you around town looking less than peachy.'

I am stunned. I want to throw my arms around his neck and squeal. Yes, I actually feel like squealing. Instead, I primly lock my fingers together and nod, as if I am a teacher and he is a particularly diligent student who has just presented me with an onerous project that he has at last, triumphantly, completed.

'George are you absolutely sure? Of course I will be your wife.' I nod in further approval. What am I thinking? 'George, you need to know then: I'm not Lily. My name is Babette. Babette Fournière.'

He looks momentarily confused as if stunned. But then appears to shake it off. How duplicitous can a little name change appear to him when he has been beset with much more profound disclosures about me?

'Pretty name, I shall have to remember that, and to get used to it. You could have told me sooner you know.' He dips into a deep bow and kisses my hand, then scoops up his hat from the hall table.

'Babette Fournière, I shall begin to make arrangements as soon as possible.' He swaggers to the door and out. I have a strong desire to jump up and down on the bed like I did as a little girl. I just don't know what to do with myself.

How should a young woman who has just been proposed to behave? I rush to the window to watch my future husband walk down the street. How handsome and assured he looks with his determined stride. Something must have distracted him … he seems to be slowing down. Now he has stopped completely. Has he forgotten something? No, I can't see anything that he may have left behind here. He's slowly looking back. Does he want to wave back to me? He doesn't. Just walks, no, more, trudges on. How very odd.

* * *

George appears to have absented himself from my life temporarily. Perhaps the enormity of having proposed to me has suddenly become a crushing burden to him. I do not want to pressure him, because I do not want him to reflect too much on his decision. As he has gone hunting this weekend, I am happy to accompany Philippe to one of the cabarets.

I am trying to be entertaining and seem to be succeeding, as our table is in very high spirits and I have been the source of some of that gaiety, but I am feeling unnerved as each time I glance to my left, a tanned and sharply elegant man is staring at me. He is standing by the bar, nursing a glass of something. He is just staring in this direction, staring with the directness of someone who appears to be on very familiar terms. Neither Philippe nor any of the others seem to have noticed him, otherwise I feel sure that someone would have commented. Philippe, I see, is not in a position to notice anything as he is happily ensconced in conversation with a young woman who is clearly trying to flatter him.

There is a gnawing feeling in my stomach, a feeling that brings me back to the early days of Madame Delphine's, to a time when I could not, dare not, bear to take in any real details of clients who had been set up for me. I learned how to fake flattery. I learned that most men respond to very basic signals and that there was no need to personalise anything. They liked submission, coyness, nothing vulgar – at least initially. They quickly tired of restraint and detachment once they began to remove their clothes. They could get enough of that at home.

At Madame Delphine's, everyone knew that there was a transaction and once the act of disrobing began, then the purchaser had rights. If I was feeling unwell, or simply tired, that was irrelevant. If their nails dug too deeply into my skin, or their brutishness left my thighs bruised or grazed, as long as it was not intended to be injurious, I had to breathe deeply and ignore it. I never encountered deliberate cruelty, but have been left sore and shaken through the sheer force of a man's lust. Often afterwards, they were spent, exhausted and irritated. Yes, strangely, even though I could feel them almost melt into my body while they steadied their breathing, they would then re-group and become a little arrogant and even sometimes a little insulting. In the early days, I found the whole business terribly confusing, and wondered if I was doing something wrong, and then I slowly realised that deep down, these men, often powerful men, resent women for the way they make them feel. They are happy to blame Eve and her wretched apple. RACHEL! Not Marie or Marthe … the maid is Rachel.

This tanned man, is this person one of those early fumblings? Oh Lord, is he actually going to be so indiscrete as to boldly march over here. I am trying to remain calm despite the pounding from my heart. Surely everyone at this table must be able to hear its thump, even over their conversation. Does he intend to so publicly proposition me? I look off at some point in the middle distance but am aware with each step, that he is closer to my side.

'Mademoiselle.' I have to look up at him. 'I am Léo.'

Philippe, though still in conversation with the pretty young woman, is aware with the keenness of a lion, that his territory has been breached and immediately raises his glass in acknowledgement of the gentleman who has just joined us. This momentarily confuses me, until I realise that of course, their paths would have crossed many times at the Madame's house.

'May I?'

Without permission given, Léo pulls up a chair at an angle to my chair. My breath catches in my throat and I am scarcely able to speak. I want to immediately hug him or prostrate myself before him in guilt, but instead I ask demurely after his well-being.

'Léo, I am so sorry about Catherine. She adored you and lived in anticipation of your return so you could begin your lives together.'

'I know. She loved you, too. A few letters found their way to me and in each, she spoke highly and lovingly of you. I wanted to meet you, because you were so important to Catherine.'

'She was constantly fretting about you, and only wanted you to come back safely.'

'I was injured and spent a few months recuperating, then when I was told about Catherine, I took myself off to the Transvaal because I heard that gold had been discovered there.'

'Well your appearance and demeanour suggest you were not entirely unlucky.'

'Catherine wrote of your friend George. She was fond of him too.'

'He is away on a hunt this weekend.'

'Why are you not with him? Although I can understand wanting to avoid the burden of some of the feminine chit-chat that consumes the dinner tables at night. I'm sure you would be bored.'

It is disconcerting that he is so familiar with the intimacies my life. But then little does he know how many tiny details Catherine had regaled to me about him. She especially liked his smell, which she described as earthy. He is close enough for me to sense what she meant. It is an outdoors forest-like mixture of oak moss and bergamot. But George's hunt?

'Is there a space for feminine chatter at these affairs? My understanding was that it was strictly a boys' pastime.'

'Well, yes, the actual hunt is. But any that I have attended, if we have close companions, wives or fiancées, they come along and are amused separately until dinner time.' He has clearly noticed my forehead creasing. 'Listen, I am probably entirely wrong and who is to say that they are all hosted similarly?'

Suddenly I am crushed that this may be the reason for this sudden and enforced separation. Might the hunt only have been a pretext? When it comes to decent company, is George being hugely disloyal to me in not wanting to have me acknowledged? Léo rises and with a slight bow, assures me how wonderful it had been to at last meet me after having only fleetingly glimpsed me before at Madame Del's.

It was Lily that he was addressing in his lowered voice. It was as Lily that I first wondered where I had come across him. And when he holds on to my hand for what seems like a second or two too long, and says that he really hopes he can see me again some time, is it to Lily that he is addressing this question? It is Lily who turns back towards the ever-generous Philippe and smiles in the untroubled way that he likes. Will she ever be truly banished?

* * *

As I step out of the carriage the air feels crisper, the moon brighter. Maybe this is why I think I can catch, just out of the corner of my eye, the shape of a man loitering nearby in a doorway. It's not the first time and I am beginning to believe that I am being followed. The stairs creak slightly under my light footstep; I want to spirit myself up them and inside my rooms as quickly as possible. It is as I fumble with my key that I feel the firm push of large hands against my back and before I can steady myself, I am tossed inside. With the door slammed shut I turn to face a bedraggled and menacing Vincent.

'The maid is just in her room.'

'No she isn't, you gave her the night off. You obviously gave poor deluded Philippe the night off too, otherwise he would be here with you now. Do you not at least owe him something for taking you to the Lapin Agile tonight and for treating you so nicely?'

I pull back my shoulders in an effort not to seem cowed. He is taller and thinner than I remembered.

'How dare you barge into my home like this? And you are drunk.'

'No, not too bad actually. Look at these plush surrounding.' He picks up a velvet cushion then tosses it aside. 'Very appropriate actually. Do you know that ladies of your occupation and standing used to be called "women in velvet"?'

I refuse to be intimidated in my own home. I walk defiantly towards him. 'I want you to leave this instant or else you will be in trouble. I promise you that.'

'Nothing left for you to do, my dear Lily. I became rather too fond of the roulette wheel since last we met. When I hastened off to Australia, I somehow managed to leave parts of my fortune in each of the territories. So I stand before you penniless and crushed. All I ever wanted from you was kindness, to give me a chance. Now, strangely, I have this urge to derail your future as mercilessly as mine has been derailed.'

I am trying hard to appear dispassionate and cold. 'How, Vincent, do you propose doing that?'

'Well, through George of course.'

I can feel a palpitation in my chest. 'George knows all about me. In fact, we are to be wed.'

'Noble that. And he still wants to marry you? He may be perfectly at peace with it. God knows, if I could lie with you I'd make peace with it too, but what about his family? You see I came across a relative of his, maverick fellow who headed to the outback in search of gold many, many years ago. He had to leave his home in disgrace. I didn't ask or care why, but the thing is, we spent a lot of time together, and I learned a lot. So I feel it my duty to pay the family a visit to reassure them about the welfare of their lost relative and to send conciliatory messages on his behalf.'

Small beads of cold sweat are now clustering just behind my fringe.

'There isn't a family around who doesn't like to hear a bit of news, a little gossip, wouldn't you think, Lily?'

'You don't scare me, and certainly you haven't a chance of holding George to any ransom.'

'Be that as it may, let me be one of the first to congratulate you.'

Before I am even aware of it, he has grabbed both of my arms and is pulling me towards him. He crushes a whiskery kiss firmly against my mouth as I struggle to push him away. I manage to free myself and shout hysterically at him to get out.

He just smirks and nods, then casually opens the door and leaves. I stand there as invaded and violated as if he had ripped all of my clothes off. Taking a seat by the fireplace, I calmly pick up my embroidery and focus on my plump woollen flowers for four stitches, before I must stop, unable to go any further. Where is George?

* * *

I don't recall sleeping, but I must have when I hear the maid clattering about trying to assemble some sort of breakfast on a tray.

'Rachel, will you do some baking today and ask your sister to help you? I want to have a dinner party tonight. In fact, I want to have a dinner party every night until George comes back. I feel like having lots of people around me.'

I spent a lovely afternoon on the Champs-Élysées ordering wine, chocolate, cakes and then consulted for half an hour with the butcher on a range of meats and fowl to be delivered over the coming days.

I only had to entertain for two evenings and happily cancelled on the third because George came home.

* * *

I have been listening to the gravel crunch of carriages and the dimming of the whip cracks as they pull away from the front of the house at regular intervals. Carriages disappear further down the tree-lined avenue leaving trails of dust clouds. I watched from my bedroom window as George's mother waved goodbye with a regal wave, her white handkerchief delicately clutched and flapping with the effort.

I am plaiting my hair into yet another elaboration while I wait for George to come and get me. Finally, the soft rap on the door and as it opens, George's head pops around it, as if asking permission for the rest of his body to enter the room.

'Just checking if you were awake.'

'My goodness, how could I not be with all the coming and going this morning. Had you many visitors?'

'Just a couple of aunts and then some cousins.'

'I feel as if I have been very rude staying up here in my room. I would have joined you all.'

'*Maman* thought you should be left to rest. She has this idea that country air fills the lungs of the city dweller in a way that they are not used to, that their sleep is longer and deeper the minute they lay their head on a pillow here.'

'Yes, but darling, there is no need to have my food sent up to me on a tray. It was very thoughtful yesterday morning but I was well rested by lunchtime and then I could hear all that laughter around the dinner table yesterday evening, which made me feel terribly left out as you can imagine. I'd very much like to join you for lunch today.'

He kisses my forehead. 'That would be lovely. I'll have a place set for you, though you will be in the company of some rather tedious neighbours who have popped around.'

He blows me a parting kiss as he closes the door behind him. Good. Now, how do I look? It is a difficult business trying to determine how best to present yourself as a future daughter-in-law. You want to give the impression, through each minute detail of your appearance, that you will be loving and reliable and discreet and a credit to the family name. This is why I have already discarded a jewel-encrusted comb that I had tucked into an earlier mound of plaited hair and have opted instead for this simple style of a low bun, pinned at the back of my neck. I am hoping that this white ruffled blouse and grey skirt with the subtle black lines, says that I am suited to life in the country and not accidentally foisted upon it. I don't know why I keep returning to the grooming habit of leaning into the mirror and smoothing my eyebrows with my middle fingers. This will hardly be a feature on which I will likely be adjudicated by George's mother. I shouldn't think that wayward eyebrows will be my downfall. Another knock and I am ready, I hope. But instead of George, a large maid bustles towards me with a weighted tray and places it on the highly polished circular table by the window which overlooks the garden.

'What is this?'

'Madame thought you would be happier having lunch in peace because some guests have dropped by unexpectedly.' The maid gives me a withering glance and turns her back to leave.

'I want you to lift this tray and bring it back downstairs with you this second. I will not be eating in my room.'

She emits a low clucking noise and lifts the tray without saying another word. I have had enough of this. Why am I even here? It was clearly on the invitation of George's family. I did not arrive unannounced like some bothersome guest who must be tolerated for the sake of manners. He promised he would introduce me to them and I was so relieved when everything was set in place. He re-assured me that this was a good thing and mocked my reluctance. My treatment so far has been, in my opinion, outrageous. Am I to remain cooped up here out of view of friend and neighbour? Am I a carrier of some vile and contagious illness? Her son loves someone who has had a past. There is little either of us can do about it.

With one final reassuring glance in the mirror, I smooth

my skirt, raise my chin and make my way down the sweeping staircase towards the conversation which is coming from behind a closed door. I open it and the men immediately stand up. Quickly seeking out George's face, I am relieved to see him smiling broadly at me as he comes towards me. With his arm lightly draped around my waist he steers me towards the table and pulls out a chair for me.

'There *Maman*, I knew Babette would be perfectly happy to join us for lunch. These are our neighbours Monsieur and Madame Gouffé, and their daughter Madeline. I'm delighted to present, Mademoiselle Babette Fournière.'

I nod graciously at the guests, reserving a slow, deliberate nod for George's mother.

'You are very welcome to our home here and I am glad you are well rested after your journey.'

George's mother, Madame Barré, fixes me with her eyes, and they are much warmer than I imagined they would be, almost friendly. George must have taken his colouring from her as her eyes are the same deep brown, her hair a glossy chestnut. Unfolding my napkin on to my lap, I declare that everything looks delicious. I have interrupted their conversation and now everyone must realign themselves to my presence as it would be completely improper to simply carry on as if I had not joined them. This, unfortunately, has the effect of me assuming the centre of attention, which is the last thing that I wanted. There is a pause, until George passes me a platter of meat and that seems to give everyone permission to resume their chattering, which is being conducted in little groupings.

'Well, what do you think of our countryside, mademoiselle?' Monsieur Gouffé is to my left and to the immediate right of George's mother who is seated at the top of the table.

'Monsieur Gouffé, I have only George's word to go on as I have not yet been in a position to soak it up yet, though I am very much looking forward to taking in the sights. It has long been a source of inspiration for him.'

'The garden here is the finest in the entire region. It is a credit to Madame Barré's patience and skill.'

'Yes, Babette, after lunch I must take you for a stroll around.'

I study her carefully to see if that invitation is being offered through gritted teeth, but on the contrary, she seems to be quite energised by the prospect.

'You smell very nice.' The small, tinkly voice is coming from my companion seated to my right, the young Mademoiselle Madeline.

'Why thank you.'

'And your bracelet is so pretty. It is so sparkling.'

'Do you think you would like to try it on?'

The young girl glances across the table at her mother.

'Now, now, Madeline. I have told you about being a nuisance at the table.'

'I'd like a bracelet like that when I'm older.'

'How old are you now?'

'I shall soon be eleven.'

'That is a very pleasant age to be.'

'Maybe my son can tell you where he purchased it. Can you, George?'

George and Mimi's eyes locked.

'No, I'm afraid I can't.'

Monsieur Gouffé chortles. 'Ah yes, I remember the old days when I had to purchase my way through several suitors. I suppose you could call it competitive purchasing. And I have since be assured that it was never the most expensive but always the most thoughtful purchases that made the greatest impression. Patience won me my prize. That would be your mother, Madeline.'

Madeline smiles broadly at both her parents. The lunch passes in random chatter, a little gossip about the antique dowager who lives on a nearby estate, some casual observations about the unseasonably warm weather and Madeline's current preference in board games. Then Madame Barré delicately rings a small bell that is sitting close to hand and the maid appears immediately.

'I think we'll serve the *soufflé* and *café* in the sunroom while I steal Babette away to show her around the garden.'

George rises from the table to pull back his mother's chair then does the same for me. As the guests file out, Madame Barré hooks my arm and leads me through the glass doors out on to the patio and into the garden. She passes me a warm wrap that she picked up from somewhere on our way from the table to the patio.

'Each little area is like a present that you come upon. This first courtyard has a strong Italian theme with this wonderful mosaic tiling and statues imported especially from Italy.'

There are enormous terracotta pots and decorative iron benches tucked into alcoves, and one huge sundial that stands taller than me. We duck under a pergola.

'This is so beautiful in June when the white jasmine is in flower. See, Babette, the way it twines through here and when you walk by, its wonderful scent completely envelopes you.'

'I am very fond of white jasmine. It is almost unbearably pretty. My mother used to pick some and place it on my pillow when I was very young.'

'It's a little untidy at the moment and needs to be tied up and supported. This is why I look forward to April. There is so much to do in a garden. If you have any hope of getting the best out of it, then you simply cannot leave it alone. Everything begins to burst into life with its early colour. You must divide your perennials and keep them well watered. Oh, and there is so much pruning to do. Look, those hydrangea stems need to be cut back and the climbers need support but then you have the promise of iris, lavender, dahlias, roses and Bougainvillea. Only, however, if you tend to things very carefully at this stage.'

Madame Barré ambles through to the Japanese garden and over to an ornate seat under the cherry blossoms. I follow closely behind. She gestures for me to sit down.

'The wonderful thing about early spring in a garden is that it is not too late to right mistakes. You can still move plants about and anything you decided was in the wrong place last year can be removed to a more suitable place without causing any damage. This is the time to sew seeds, to look forward and prepare for the season ahead. Do you really love George, Babette?'

I as startled at this.

'With all my heart Madame Barré.'

'And I do not doubt that for one second. Nor do I doubt George's love for you which is why I must put pressure on you.'

'What's wrong, Madame? Tell me.'

'George cannot marry you. He, however, will never, ever come to that conclusion himself, which is why you must make the decision for him. Babette, this is our home and it has remained in this family for generations. George's father is ill and does not have long left to live. George will be expected to take over his father's responsibilities and that includes the upkeep of everything you see around you here. He can only do that if he marries someone with wealth of her own. There are several young ladies his father and I have identified over the years and one in particular that I know George is very fond of, and in time, could grow to love. But it will never happen if you are in his life.'

I feel embarrassed as tears begin to sting my eyes.

'You are a bright and lovely girl, and I can understand George's feelings for you entirely, but only you can do what is best for him. Only you have that power. Come, let me show you the orangery. It is so peaceful and everything has such promise when you spend time in it.'

We walk in silence up several foot-worn steps, each one lined with a potted plant. A gravel path swirls around a large fountain where marble cherubs poise mid-frolic, their white, dimpled hands perpetually grasping skyward. Madame Barré flings open the high doors of the gleaming, glass house at the top of the path and we both step into its warmth. My heels clip the black and white tiled floor.

'I love to sit here among the potted orange and lemon trees and the early blooms. Even all these busts of old Roman men have become reassuring company to me over the years.'

I stroll behind Madame Barré like an unwilling student of horticulture trying to feign attentiveness while my mind has, in fact, taken flight. Her directive, for that is what it was and not the entreaty that she packaged up and so delicately presented to me, is like an unpleasant echo resonating around my skull. 'Cannot marry you. Cannot marry you.'

'… or "Devil's Trumpet", as it's more commonly known.'

'I'm sorry, what was that? That plant there?'

'This broad leafed plant, *Datura Stramonium*. It flowers later in the summer as a long white trumpet shape.'

Datura. I am transported back to the heavy rich red curtains which opened on my very first opera. That thrilling

first flush as those sweet sounds from *Lakmé* and her servant
Mallika and Lakmé's lover, floated upward, like petals dancing on a gentle perfumed breeze, how I clasped the edge of
my seat in awe while Philippe patiently guided me through
this new world, how I glanced across to the next box where
my eyes fell on George.

'It is a lovely garden. Your patience shines through. Do you
mind if I stroll a little on my own, Madame Barré? I am
trying to instruct myself in the art of perfumery.'

'Of course.' She smiles and leaves me. I watch as she bends
down to tug at a weed, discard it and then wipe her hands
briskly in satisfaction.

WARM VANILLA

Maurice looks so peaceful as I rock him. Maria is preparing some lunch and the stove crackles with freshly tossed kindling. This new apartment of hers is much more spacious and I'm relieved that living here in Rue Tourlaque keeps her close by to me. Old Madame Valadon has completely taken charge of the baby in an effort to speed Maria back to her modelling jobs. It was through a painter friend, that Maria had managed to find these rooms for her baby and her mother.

The three rooms they all occupy are more pleasant than the Rue Poteau apartment and the general atmosphere is very lively as the building is home to several artists. However, Maria looks exhausted.

'Would you believe my mother is now absolutely intent on trying to find me a husband? The pressure is unbearable.'

'I think she just worries about you.'

'You mean she worries about herself.'

'Has she any candidates in mind?'

'Don't laugh, but she's convinced Henri could be the one.'

'Hmmm, you and Lautrec, I'm not so sure about that. Can you imagine how short your children would be?'

She flicks a cloth at me in mock annoyance.

'He is being so odd with me these days. I think he's a little jealous that so much of my time is being taken up.'

'Never mind him. What about your drawing? You must be building up a nice collection by now.'

'It's funny. I now have a lot more space to draw and a lot less time.'

Maria lifts Maurice from my arms as he is beginning to get restless.

'I have to get back to modelling as soon as possible to bring some money in. I've been doing a little. I look at the new art schools springing up and those wealthy young ladies with all the leisure time in the world to indulge in painting, and I can't tell you how maddening it is. It just isn't fair.'

She rocks Maurice and stirs a pot with a large wooden spoon at the same time.

'Come May when the Salon opens again, we must go and take a look at Puvis de Chavanne's painting, *The Sacred Wood*. That large one I modelled for. Took forever, but at least he is helping me with my rent.'

I quickly glance at Maurice. Maria had spent a lot of time with Puvis at his studio in Neuilly and fell pregnant not long after. But Puvis must be at least thirty, maybe forty years older than her. Then again, Maria had also been spending a lot of time in the company of a handsome, swarthy man, whose particular talent was a mesmerising, traditional candle dance that he performed at the Chat Noir. I was dragged along and could not understand Maria's newly discovered fascination with candle dancing, until I too watched him. But suddenly, he was gone, off travelling around other parts of Europe and little else was spoken of him. If my friend remains unconcerned about Maurice's parentage, then it is pointless me wasting my time in speculation.

Maria is now walking around the room speaking in a very animated way while swinging Maurice as he lies on his tummy across her arms.

'Have you come across Seurat yet? Or Redon? They are doing incredible things with colour and form. It is thrilling.'

'Maria, look, Maurice has fallen asleep again.'

'Oh, thank God.' She tucks him into his cradle. 'Now *Maman* will probably come crashing in with her brandy breath and wake him up.'

Maria stokes the fire and closes the stove door. She then reaches for a bottle of wine and two glasses.

'It's all so exhausting. I'd love to just escape.'

'Wine and Hashish, Baudelaire apparently swore by it. Was that to escape or to become an exalted version of yourself? I can't remember.'

'Wine will do, unless you happen to have an opium pipe on you.'

I pat myself down and shrug.

'It will be fine. I'll tour the cafés and the dance-halls as soon as I get a bit more strength, then I'm back to my drawing. I'll produce some masterpieces. I'll become the darling of the *Salon* and live in a magnificent and obscenely large apartment somewhere in the seventeenth arrondissement with an enormous studio just on the other side of the hall.'

'What you need is to sleep. Do that while Maurice is asleep, otherwise you will look like the walking dead, and that is not a good look for a girl on the prowl for a husband.'

'It's my mother who is on the prowl for a husband, not me.'

A large folder rests near my elbow. I flick it open. There are only a couple of drawings in it: a self-portrait in pastel and a charcoal drawing of her mother in profile.

'Maria, where are all the drawings you showed me before?'

My friend is suddenly transfixed by the light of the stove.

'Maria?' She continues to stare, then shudders a little.

'It was some time in early January, Maurice was only a few days old and the snow ... it seemed as if it would never stop. The baby was turning purple because he was so cold and there's only so much warmth both of us can get from one shawl. The thing is, I had burned everything that could be burned. Almost everything.'

She gives her battered folder a little nudge. 'Except some of this. I tossed them, one by one, into the fire.'

I am not sure if I am more struck by her foolishness, or stunned by her selflessness. In that moment, she had condemned herself to a life of drudgery and struggle. As if those sketches would only taunt her, only remind her of unfulfilled ambition.

'When I came to these final two, I stopped myself. It's hard to explain. I signed one of them "Suzanne V" and in a way, with that new signature, I was dedicating myself to the life of an artist. I watched my work disappear into ash and made myself that promise.'

She smiles, almost apologetically, but I feel consumed in a wave of admiration for her. This beautiful, talented, committed young woman, only slightly younger than I am, she has made a declaration, quietly and without fuss. I get up from my chair. I must go and find my mother.

* * *

With blood pounding in my head, so vividly I can almost taste it, I doggedly traipse through the city until I am standing in front of the formidable sprawl of a building, the place that is nicknamed, 'Pox-victims Bastille'. They refuse to allow me entry and I am firmly rebuffed by the guard at the door. Peering through the fence of the large exercise yard, I'm sure I must soon be able to see some of the patients who are brought out for fresh air in the morning. I am determined to be there from the moment their daily routine begins until their day draws to an end so that I might catch a glimpse of my mother. There is nothing for it but to tuck myself tightly into the corner of a doorway. I fasten every button on my jacket and pull my woollen shawl around me and try to sleep.

The forceful nudge of the large wooden door jolts me awake. The guard, on realising that I am the impediment to the execution of his normal morning routine, shouts at me and tries to haul me up from the ground, which he is perfectly within his rights to do. I do, however, find myself screaming furiously that I am not going to move until I see my mother. He clasps his large hand easily around my arm and pulls me up and away from the doorway. I try to soften my tone. He must deal with mad women every day and even in my anxiety, I realise that reason will be best served here. But it is too late. All that is in front of him, as far as he is concerned, is an annoyance and a hindrance. He brushes past hard against my shoulder as if brute force will shatter me into particles that the wind will carry off.

'Please, I only need a few minutes.'

My pleading may be that of a hungry alley cat for all the humanity that he is displaying. A man steps around us briskly, but then stops and turns to look back.

'Fleur?'

The guard shoves me a little towards the man.

'You know her! Then get her away from here.'

I raise my hand to shield my eyes from the sharp morning sun and try to determine who is speaking.

'Fleur. It's me, Gaston, George's friend. Leave her. I've got her.'

On seeing him, I am suddenly aware of feeling embarrassed. He folds me into his side, covering me slightly with his coat and eases me across to the other side of the road.

'Come, we'll go into this café.'

He finds a small corner table by the window and sits me down while ordering two brandies. In the warmth of the café and the purposeful intent of people going about their everyday business, and the dishevelled reflection that I realise must be me, I shake my head – no my entire being – as if trying to jolt myself from a bad dream. The drinks are quickly delivered and I cup both hands around the bulbous glass.

'I'm sorry, look at the state of my nails.'

I gulp down the brandy and Gaston clicks for another immediately.

'Fleur, how did you get like this? You look in such a dreadful state.'

The brandy just adds to the layer of fog in my mind. Nothing feels vivid.

'Gaston, I've made a terrible mistake. I thought I was helping my mother, she is very ill, and now I've condemned her to that hell over there.'

He glances over towards the imposing building.

'I don't know what to do. I need to get her out of there. She will die.'

'Fleur, you will destroy your own health by hanging around there. You're freezing and you look terrible. And when did you last have a decent meal?'

This makes me smile. 'I had some meringue, was it two, maybe three days ago?'

'Let me get you some food.'

And soon, before me, there is coffee and breads and mackerel and cheese. A desperate combination of sustenance, some of which he clearly hopes I will pick at. And I do. And it feels good to have different tastes on my tongue and soon the layers of fog dissipate and there is a clearing.

'Are you feeling a little better?'

I nod sheepishly. For the first time, Gaston sits back in his chair, in the relaxed attitude more befitting of a coffee and small meal between friends. As he reclines, I am aware of how fresh smelling he is, as if he has just bathed in a tub of warm milk infused with vanilla. Everything about me, by contrast, is crusted and caked. My hair hangs in lank twists. The smell of my body evaporates through my damp clothes, but Gaston is pretending not to notice.

'Glad to be of help, at least to someone, because George is not paying any attention to me or to anything.'

George. A piece of bread seems to have become drier and harder to swallow at the sound of George's name. My mind is now clear enough to feign a detached interest in Gaston's difficulty with his friend. Maybe I can even be of help.

'Is he being obstinate about something?'

'Someone, more likely. I have warned him it will end badly, but he is blinded. He thinks it is love, but it is more obsession, or, you're right, obstinacy.'

I indicate a 'carry on' signal with my raised fork, for in truth, I seem to have lost the ability to formulate actual words.

'They both must know the ways of the world, and setting her up in a nice apartment in Paris, then ensuring he has lots of business to conduct here…well, that should be how it's done.' Gaston cuts into something on his plate, I am unsure what. 'I've said to him, you know, pointed it out, that his great-aunt Eugenie, the one who bequeathed the property to her direct descendants, enormous portrait hanging on the first landing and all that, well even though she's long dead, her opinions still hold a lot of sway, and she was the one who practically invented the class system.'

I am digesting and shamefully relishing the dilemma as it unfolds.

'So she is not suitable for George then, do you think?'

He leans forward, both hands now clasped.

'Of course she is beautiful, well so he expounds elaborately and effusively. The more he drinks, the more divine this creature becomes, but the Barrés would not countenance their lineage being sullied by a … a courtesan.'

I gasp and lower my fork.

'I have been trying to state the obvious to him, that the inheritance is through the mother's line and his father does not have a healthy enough income to maintain the estate, that unless he wants to toss his mother out into some cobbler's cottage, he is going to have to do what he has been raised to do. This interlude here in Paris … I said to him to consider himself merely a soldier on furlough and his regiment is now calling him back to duty.'

He swirls what remains of the cognac in his glass.

'And Adèle is a beautiful, accomplished girl, so all is not lost.'

'Adèle?'

'George is being dismissive of her because she is his cousin, but it's so far removed it hardly counts. He knows she was being groomed for him. It is a pickle of a situation. He can't see past Babette, bless him.'

'Babette? Her name is Babette?'

'That's right!' He thumps the table. 'Of course, I forget that you all had that intrigue and caper. The – what was it – the dead painter and evaporation of the model into thin air? Forgot that.'

'She was in prison. She went home. We, George and I, we went to the prison and we were told that.'

'Yes, that whole prison episode, apparently it was down to an over-zealous policeman who was trying to inflate his quotas for the incarceration of undesirables and vagrants and the unregistered. Several were released when it was discovered. But she did end up in a brothel, one of the better ones mind you. My own uncle is rather partial to it.'

'He met her at a brothel?'

'No, no. Some other story behind it. God knows. But he is that stubborn, it didn't change anything when he found out. I am telling you, this is not going to end well.'

I can only stare out of the window. I am lost for any kind of rejoinder: humorous, shocked, observational. There is nothing. I have been struck as if dumb.

'Fleur', he follows my gaze. 'Perhaps your mother needs to be over there. Maybe it's for her own good.'

I stand up with such ferocity that my chair scrapes loudly back on the wooden floor.

'I thank you for your generous drink, for your kindness, for the food, but I will also thank you to keep your opinions to yourself. I know my mother. I know what's best for her, and over there …' I emphasise by jabbing angrily at the window, 'over there is not it.'

Gulping down the last drop of brandy, I march out the door glancing briefly back at Gaston. He looks utterly bewildered.

* * *

It is numbing how quickly you can lose your sense of dignity. I have a doorway corner that is becoming so familiar to me that I know how best to angle my head against the ridges of the wood. Last night, I actually wept because I did not take enough care with the cobweb that had been delicately embroidered above the hinges, and I tore it asunder with one careless sweep of my arm. I felt as if I had committed an act of murder. I felt as if a close friend had died. I felt as if I had betrayed something, some code of conduct that only the street dweller understands.

Babette and me. Two paint splodges, one painter's bristled brush. We bleed each others hues and splatter on his canvas. Visceral daubings. When I close my eyes, we are swirling pigments of blues and yellows, then he slashes through us with his palette knife and renders us green. Each night I dream of green; at first meadow fresh where daisies bob, then battered and storm-sliced, then moulding and putrid. And in that green decay, I have lost Babette. I have lost me. We are neither of us.

The rim of the wood indents me, and prods me daily to reluctant wakefulness, at least partially so. Slowly, as each grain of dirt and grime cloaks my skin, I become encased and it's almost comforting. You cannot scrape at me; I am numb I tell you. I am not even sure my blood is still flowing. I cut myself, deeply, just to reassure myself that I could still feel, but as I stared blankly at the deep crimson forking down towards my fingers, it proved nothing.

And people move around me, and I am this detached nothingness. Is it my blackness? I shouldn't look them in the eye. I am a dark pit that the kindest of them might tumble into, and be consumed.

She is not suffering – that fat woman with the brown stumps of teeth. She sits in that doorway as she earnestly de-fleas a cat that she had locked between her legs. It is a hateful cat. It spits and snarls. She should fling it against the wall so we could both watch it slide down into a crumpled, gut-spilled heap.

Shuffle. Shuffle. Slush shuffle. More cloth to bind my boots. Hunched. 'Straight back.' If she could see me now, she would be cross. 'Stand up straight.' But she can't. And I can't see her. 'Straight back', she shouted once when I was younger and flailing, and I straightened it immediately, and what she meant was, 'No dawdling'. A snatch. I am filled with snatches of recall. Tobacco whirls, tapping cane. Her sewing in the garden. Then rough hands, hands that were trusted but then betrayed. Snatches, like a slightly cracked window into a stuffy room.

Almost extinguished, edge-singed and then new-born scream, and life was something vital again. It pulsed before me and was briefly sweet.

Clawing. Clawing. Maggot earth.

Would anyone notice if I faded? I want to. I am beyond consolation. Day to night, night to day again. It will be a release.

'Fleur. Fleur.'

Stop shaking me. Leave me be.

'Fleur.'

I look up. A shimmering spectre dotted by sun-spots leaks through my splayed fingers. He leans down, another figure standing solidly behind him.

'Fleur, it's me. It's George.'

It's George. George. I think I smile. I feel hands under my arm-pits and I am on my feet. Gaston vigorously rubs my shoulders and arms. I turn to the fence of the hospital yard.

'I'm waiting for my mother.'

'Fleur, listen to me. Gaston's uncle is an influential doctor. He will take care of your mother.' He indicates to his coat pocket. 'I can get her released. I have papers. I'll go speak to them.'

Something stirs me to wakefulness. I watch as George goes into the building. I am in no state to be seen in official company. I imagine him speaking sternly to the grumpy, sweating man with a large bunch of keys who will be sitting in a squalid cluttered office. He will probably ask George to follow him down long corridors through wailing and hollow-eyed stares. The guard will scan the dozens and dozens of ragged gowns and grimy bonnets until his eyes fall on the slight figure of my mother who is probably standing all alone, perhaps rocking herself. I have watched as they do this on their morning exercises. I have begun to do it myself. I am afraid to breathe. Gaston stands further back. As both of us staring at the door, George returns with a smile.

'It is done. She needs to be looked over first and some paperwork must be completed but we can come back for her.'

I hear soft, stuttering sobs that melt into a seamless weep. I realise it is me. I feel relief. I feel.

* * *

Dr Philippe's office has shelves and shelves of books. There are marble busts on plinths and the red walls are hung with several large paintings. His huge oak desk dominates the centre of the room and there are plump leather chairs with brass studs and a patterned chaise-longue with a matching large pillow, smaller pillow and bolster stacked against the head of it. I sit waiting while *Maman* dresses behind the screen. Dr Philippe pours water from a jug into a bowl, then taps his hands dry on a white linen towel. Long, bony but delicate fingers.

'That, Mademoiselle, is for the study of phrenology.'

I have been staring at a white ceramic head, sectioned off into numbers and words. He motions me over to the velvet-draped plinth where it is resting like a guillotined trophy.

'The head is divided up into twenty-seven different sections or brain organs. See this section, section four. That is a person's instinct for self-defence and courage. Number nine: vanity, ambition, love of glory. Number twelve: the sense of places, of space proportions, of time. Number thirteen: the memory of people, the sense of people. Number eleven: the memory of facts, the memory of things. Look here at number five: even the propensity for committing murder. Everything is mapped out in the bumps of a person's head.'

He steps close to me and takes both sides of my head in the palms of his hands. I stare up into his grey eyes as he concentrates, feeling the shape of my skull, tracing it with his thumbs and fingers. He slowly tilts it back. For a few seconds, it is almost as though he is going to kiss me. His hands spring away.

'Ah, Madame Delphy, come sit down here.' He pats the back of the chair and takes his seat behind his desk.

'Madame, I'm going to give you a potassium tartrate of iron pills, and I recommend this oak bark. I shall also prescribe an ointment to be applied three times daily. Fleur will you be able to oversee all this?'

I nod obediently.

'We'll hold off on the opium until I can monitor you some more and in the meantime, plenty of fresh air, preferably sea air if you can manage it.'

'Thank you so much doctor, I really …'

'Now your turn, Mademoiselle. Mademoiselle, I need you to concentrate. I don't like the sound of that rattle in your chest. You'll need all your strength to take care of your mother. I want you to wrap up warm, take plenty of ginger and make up a warm poultice of garlic and onion which you need to apply to your throat. George tells me he has arranged for you both to stay in the country to recuperate and I think that's a good idea. Come back to me in six weeks, unless there are any dramatic developments in the meantime.'

My mother rises slowly to her feet. She seems to have little notion of where she is, but still manages a small, gracious curtsey to the gentleman who is being so kind to her. Dr Philippe holds the door open for us as we leave.

* * *

The country is very still. When you are hemmed by buildings and funnelled down streets, sometimes you forget to just be still and breathe. When you are in a city, you live life in a clatter of trams and trains and talk. It is so easy to lose yourself in all the busyness. But here, as I pick my way through a light mottled forest and listen for the crack of twig underfoot, I feel as if I am in the centre of the world, both fortified and freed, a delicate branch at the top of the highest tree, decorated in cloud wisps.

These past few days have been restorative. The first nights here before my fever broke, were sweat drenched as strange and violent dreams hacked through me. But now, I am flooded with calm, as surely as if I had been flushed through with the purest of spring water. Anything rancid and fetid has somehow been dislodged from within me and even my lungs have responded with glorious, chest-swelling exhilaration. I take a deep breath.

Walking with George has helped. Trying to frame Babette, the patchouli girl, within some sort of narrative has been difficult. I am doing my best to feign astonishment and delight for George. With my new clarity of thought, I am well aware, however, that my honest instinct is to wish grim things would befall her, leaving George and I in unimpeded bliss. But that was never meant to be. So I was not entirely disappointed when I heard that she had been feeling a little unwell and unable to join us.

'After all my effort, George! I shouldn't have just waited around and presumed a beautiful young woman like Babette, would have been blown into your path somehow.'

'You could have knocked me over with a feather when everything dawned on me. You have no idea, Fleur.'

I am slightly derailed by his reference to a feather. It saddens me that he didn't say it knowingly, that it didn't resonate with him in the same way it did with me, that a feather was his introduction one afternoon at the Café Guerbois and already it served as no point of reference for him. He clearly has no memory of it.

'Fleur, you could have died from exposure through sheer stubbornness if Gaston hadn't stumbled across you.'

I shrug. I am feeling foolish. I would like to think I had taken a principled stance whereas what I know is that I had arrived at a complete point of abdication. It was a withdrawal. I was beyond reach. Beyond compassion. I cannot fathom it. That fragility has left me, as I walk, arm linked, his hunting tweeds damp and smelling of tobacco.

'My family has cut me off, and I am now struggling a little.'

George has not yet volunteered the information about

Babette's occupation, but I am certain that this is the source of his family's ultimatum.

'I am sure ultimately, my family's innate decency will win through. They must know that the preservation of a rather grand set of walls, should not trump a person's happiness.'

'Are they fond of Babette?'

He grins and squeezes my arm. 'How could they not be? She will triumph in the end, through all the obstacles. I can promise you that.'

'George, Gaston spoke a little of this. There does seem to be a lot at stake here, and there must be a certain amount of sympathy for your family's … concern.'

'Babette is feeling enormous regret about it all. But she is convinced we will get through this. She does have a little inheritance, money put aside for herself and her sisters, and has offered to try to raise a loan against it, which I will not allow.'

I am sure that Babette has been shrewd and has accumulated assets. There must be jewellery, and furnishings and probably trunk loads of clothes that she would be unable to get through in a lifetime. George seems deflated, world weary. I would pawn my last possession for him.

'And what about her family?'

'Yes, some type of falling out. But she feels now, though it fills her with horror, that she should go and visit them. There is an older sister with a child that she especially dreads thinking of, but one day there should be a troop of little cousins running around, so bridges do need to be mended. Her family are getting impatient with letters and have been instructing her to come back. Her father, apparently, never got over the shock of having two daughters and no sons, so he seems indifferent by all accounts.'

Family ties, they can be so difficult. *Maman*, like me, has been enjoying walks in the fresh air, especially in the garden. Her health is improving, but her mind? Her minds hangs together as delicately as a cobweb. She is very confused. She keeps asking after my father. Then in the evening, she sits by the fire, calmly engaged in the act of sewing, her graceful fingers tugging at invisible threads and wrestling imaginary needles through fanciful pieces of cloth, a mesmerising and elegant motion.

The garden boy who lives in a cottage near the estate found her wandering in her bare feet late at night, looking, she said, for fallen apples to bake a pie for her husband. She had scooped up her apron by both corners and filled it with small rocks. He steered her gently back to the house and even carried her rocks for her, placing them carefully on the long wooden kitchen table.

These walks with George … is there no way we could just seal ourselves into the here and now? Could we be stitched into one huge tapestry then safely hung for all to admire? Is there any ruse by which I could keep him here for just a little longer? The place I have felt most safe in a very long time is right here, my arm linked on to his.

SOURED MILK

George has been cut off. I am sure that I can raise several thousand francs by disposing of a lot of my things. I know he is trying to appear unperturbed, but there is a lot at stake here. Vincent was true to his word and barely broke breath before rushing to the Barrés home on his 'sociable' visit, bringing with him all manner of 'family news'. This is difficult. George's mother, when I think about it, could not have been more lethally proficient had she simply pushed me over the nearest cliff.

'More tea, sister?'

How is it possible to so despise your own flesh and blood? We were close growing up. She was much more adventurous than I, and always climbed that higher branch at the most severe risk to her petticoat. I was too self-aware. My distress at getting mud on my boots was beyond reason. An ill-fitting bonnet left me inconsolable. I think I may have been told I was pretty once too often, and it left me in a state of severe anxiety as I felt constantly beholden to this birthright of mine. If I did not honour it, and tend to it, it would be snatched away, or dissolve and what would I be left with? Certainly not courage.

It did not impact on my father one way or the other, the fact that people smiled warmly at me and talked of me as though I wasn't even there. It was always in pleasant terms. Large-busted women with folded arms would cackle approval as I passed by and then smile at my father. This didn't seem to make him proud, for all we were to him were two daughters, when a son would have been much more bountiful. Had we been two sons? Well, heaven's multitude of blessings would have enriched his life beyond his wildest dreams!

And mother? What a strange and ambivalent relationship a woman has to her daughters. As babies and toddlers, we reflect on her everything that is good and godly. She is a beautiful and revered Madonna and her status secured. As the daughters grow older and blossom, they become instead something against which she measures herself. It become all about loss. Loss of youth, loss of beauty and appeal. We must appear as leeches, sucking the very essence of her woman-hood. She withers to our bloom. Sometimes I catch a look in her eye. Once when I twirled in delight in an especially gorgeous gown, purple I remember, there was something in her gaze, a kind of hardness. And maybe my father's seeming disinterest in us, in me in particular, was out of some pro-found sense of kindness to my mother and to the times, long before, when she once twirled for him.

They say that beauty is a trap, but I was entrapped. I was much too young to have to learn its lessons. They say that beauty is captivating, but I was its captive. It terrorised me for years. My uncle warned me that boys and men would want to touch me and that I must be very, very careful. He instilled in me the rampant beastliness of men as he unbuttoned his trousers, because he loved me, he told me, and did not want me to be curious about a man's body. It was confusing, as if I was petting an old turkey's neck that bobbed lightly to my childish touch. But it was to be our secret, of course.

'If you would pass me the sugar please?'

My sister primly lifts the silver tongs and places two cubes into my cup. I haven't taken two cubes for many years now, but she does not pause to verify if there have been any changes in my life, in my preferences, in my world view, in my taste in tea.

And *le bébé* scrambles about my ankles like a demented simian. His cheeks enflamed, his tiny nostrils trying to flare through crusted mucus. She seems no more enchanted by him than I, and nods ferociously to her maid to bundle him up and remove him. She puckers into a pretend kiss as her son looks pleadingly at her over the milk-stained shoulder of the maid. The mouth drops open just a little, then wider than I imagined possible. The head is thrown back in howling anguish. His bouncing wails can be heard disappearing down the hall.

'When are we likely to meet him, this George of yours?'

'Very soon, hopefully.'

'Will you not stay longer with mother and father? I do my very best, and they often say they would be lost without me, because they do value my company, but my time is very filled up with the baby and the house.'

Even if I did want to stay longer at home, doing so would appear to be of benefit to my sister, which makes me want to leave immediately. What is it that has annoyed me so much about her over the passing of the years, to have me at the stage where I would like to slap her, mid-sentence? We used to have proper conversations, but now the inane drivel is nothing but an irritant. We even got drunk once together when she spirited a bottle of something or other away from the confines of a cabinet. Neither of us knew what it was, but as we sat under the apple tree swigging vile mouthfuls it was truly us against the world.

I think it was her defeat. Her feeble surrender to expectation and conformity that so appalled me. She yielded to notions of acceptable female behaviour with total compliance, in what seemed like a heartbeat. But worse than that, she became judgemental. And when she snared a weak-chinned man of impressive earning power, she became insufferable.

I am beginning to become weighed down in the minutiae of curtain patterns as I think, at least from what I can make out, that the windows are soon to be seasonally dressed. I am fearful that my opinion will be sought for I have not been paying sufficient attention. Perhaps part of my acute discomfort is that in many ways, I dread I am not that far removed from my sister. I have been known to become excited by the trivial, and it is something I must fight against It would be a horror to drive George into the same eye-rolling irritation that her husband exhibits. She doesn't even notice. She seems oblivious to the knee bounce that tells me he could snap the head of the nearest ornament through sheer frustration. In fact he absented himself at the earliest possible convenience to attend to some frightfully important papers in his office.

More than anything, amid the twittering on the relative merits of gold tassels or fringes, I am trying to think about George, and what I am to do. It could be so perfect, if we were to stay locked away in an apartment on a Parisian boulevard. If we could repel the sharp blade of George's circumstances before it slices our dreams to shreds. I feel its jab and doubt my armour. He believes he can steed charge its reality away.

He trusts his exuberance will save the day, which is clearly why his mother had to initiate me into the conspiracy of his salvation. It was an unfair thing to do. Whose advice can I seek? Whose soundings can I trust? My heart tells me that all but George should just be damned to hell and to chance.

I am leaning towards the idea of asking Fleur and for her opinion. But she was just a random girl who I foolishly sought out in my weakened state. George told me that she had been very keen to find me, but that could be just fanciful talk on his part. I am sure she would have little recollection of me. He has promised that we will all meet up, and I would find that very interesting. I shall bring her a gift.

'... and that's why the brocade must be replaced.'

Dear Lord, are we still talking about curtains? My brain has atrophied.

CINNAMON CHOCOLATE

The carriage ride to the Maison de Santé is almost unbearable. *Maman* is excited by all the pretty fields and wild flowers and is not thinking about her destination. It is very well run, from what I have been assured, and the patients – or inmates – can exercise in plenty of large open spaces within its walls. Her hand is as soft as buttery pastry that could melt any second. The lane up to the main entrance is wide and tree lined. We are greeted by the doctor in charge who looks to be a kindly man with a huge white bushy beard.

'You can settle her in her room, Fleur. But be patient and explain to her where she is and why she is here. You do not want your mother to feel deceived in any way, because she will remember and could hold a grudge against you and it could interfere with her care here.'

I do my best to reassure her that though she is ill, the doctors will be able to help make her mentally stronger and will relieve her stress. I cannot determine if she has grasped what I am trying to tell her in any way.

Her room is white and smells of starch but there is a vase of fresh flowers on the windowsill and a lovely view of the rolling hills. The fresh air catches her grey wisps. I want to believe that she approves and understands. She sits on her bed, her feet flat and firm on the polished floor, her hands clasped on her lap. She looks docile. She looks trusting and resigned.

* * *

Back in Montmartre, I am feeling much stronger. The apartment needs airing out as there is a stale neglected smell about it. I fold away *Maman*'s things and scrub the windows and scoop out the corners and generally try to put some order on the place. It has the squalor that is often associated with a disquiet mind. Some women obsessively clean when they are feeling out of sorts or disturbed and I feel it a pity that this particular affliction has managed to pass me by, for at least my home would have benefited from my discord.

A soft rapping draws me to the window and peering out through its newly buffed glean, I can see the ruddy cheeks of young Joseph.

'A fat gentleman told me to keep him informed about when you got back and to give you this when you did.'

'Joseph, how did you know I moved here?'

'That's my job, mademoiselle. Everybody's business is mine.'

Turning on his heels and with hands plunged deep in his pockets, he meanders off into a side street. Job done. I recognise Walrus's hand.

My dear Mademoiselle,
I'll expect you and your delicate palate at the entrance of

the Café de Foy this evening at 5:30 p.m. precisely. We shall further your education by trawling the cafés and restaurants of the Palais Royal.

In friendship,
J.C. Mitoire

My light blue dress with the contrasting underskirt and matching basque makes me appear almost presentable. If there wasn't a colour clash, I would wear the green velvet hat with now only the merest hint of patchouli still crushed in its folds. I have been treating it almost as an object of worship, as if it possessed enchanted powers. It is a hat, belonging to a girl who, in the blink of an eye, has whipped my foolish imaginings into submission. No, I shall wear it. It fits me perfectly, as if it always belonged to me. I also found the matching white glove to the one that I clutched in my sleep-walking, dream-fevered state. A pair of white gloves. I can only think that Babette must have left them here also, along with her hat. I pull them on and they too fit perfectly. My mother's emerald broach will marry the colours together. It is of course not emerald, but coloured glass.

I stride purposefully to the Palais Royal, convincing myself that onlookers are admiring my coordinated style. I resolve to remain immune to the reflexive scrutiny of those who, at a glance, know coloured glass from precious stone.

Walrus tips his hat and leads me into the first restaurant where we sit down to a bowl of mock turtle soup.

If I thought I was settling in for the evening, I was mistaken; for no sooner is the soup finished than he indicates that we are setting off for the next course at another restaurant. He does not encourage me to remember the names of the restaurants and cafés, just the way their food is served. One of the venues is so elegant with its dark, charred beams; another is elaborate with stucco walls and Grecian statues, while a third has long mirrors and crimson upholstery. Next we enter one which has a private room upstairs where courtesans can be entertained with discretion.

I am whisked from a noisy café which serves a delicious garlic *ragoût*, to the reverential silence of another where we slowly and delicately cut our way through a dish of quail stuffed with thrush stuffed with lark, layer by sumptuous layer.

I mirror Walrus in the languid appreciation with which he cuts into each morsel, identifying single flavours then luxuriating in the juices of the meat. We lift our forks to our mouths in studied unison and it comes as a revelation to me: food is enjoyed all the more as a shared experience. It ceases to be merely functional and is instead a communion. Walrus closes his eyes and emits a small moan of sheer pleasure with each raise of his fork. He tells me about a truly great meal which is made by placing a quail inside a partridge which is placed inside a duck and this then would be cooked inside a pheasant which itself would have been used to stuff a goose. Such abundance could spiral me into an over-wrought state.

At the next establishment, I just about manage the individual potted pastry desserts made with the meringue topping, before we move on to a small café where we have coffee and a selection of almond and cinnamon biscuits. Finally we visit a little place which Walrus declares sells the best ice cream in the world. I decline the visit to a lively café where, he implores, we would drink sweet wine and finish with a sampling of cheeses. The trip to the master chocolatier will also have to be put back to another day as I try to settle my stomach with a small liqueur. Walrus beams in contentment and laughs at my surrender.

Easing my way home, I nod to the young streetwalkers as I do on most occasions. I like to make a comment or two about the cool night air or the dampness of the morning by way of conversation, just to make them feel engaged and not merely objects for display.

'It could snow again before spring is out.'

The young girl paces the same small stretch of pavement several times a week.

'Oh, I hope not. We're not allowed to wear warm undergarments … not good for the customer's convenience, don't you know.' She laughs giddily as she tosses some stray hair off her shoulders. I step closer to her.

'I know you from somewhere.'

The young girl shrugs her shoulders. 'Well, my boot leather is being worn thin along this path for the past few weeks now.'

That's not it. I study her more closely. She has filled out slightly and looks older but this young prostitute is the little girl I had stumbled across at Molière's circus.

'I saw you once, with your grandmother.'

The young girl's cockiness slips, and she drops her head slightly. 'My poor *grand-mère*. She died of tuberculosis. Did you know her?'

Oh God, another sullied soul. Another mind corrupted and defiled. Another path diverted into the tangled undergrowth. I should have tried harder with her. I should have stood up to them all.

'What's your name?'

'Listen, I have work to be doing, and if you keep me dawdling here any longer. Just go.'

'I'm sorry. Of course, I don't want to get you into any trouble. But do you remember someone bursting in on you when you were with your grandmother at the circus in the Bois de Boulogne? Your grandmother was very angry with me, but I was looking for someone else, and I'm sorry, it was none of my business.'

'You? What, are you determined to shadow me or something?' The young girl's eyes narrow in anger. I remember that same look in the eyes of her grandmother.

'No, you don't understand.'

'Leave me alone, or I'm going to end up with my face slashed.'

I can't help myself. I take her by the shoulders and shake her. 'Get out of this life. Don't let them destroy you.'

Her slap against my cheek is forceful. She pulls away from me and continues walking with the same indolent pace of all the other prostitutes on the darkened lane, as if she did not have a care in the world.

* * *

I wait while Agnes patiently fusses the last of her customers out of her café door, returning hats to them, retrieving forgotten umbrellas for them, until finally she can close the shutters to signal that delicious moment of pause when a busy working day has ended. She seems tired as I pour two glasses of beer and pull back a chair for her. She touches my cheek with her hand. I feel its calluses scrape against me ever so slightly. I have come to realise that her high vivacious moods are often swiftly followed by a crashing melancholy, almost as visible and cloying as the rolling mists over the Place du Tertre. She has been too fond of laudanum in the past and I suspect that it has begun to rob her of her reason again.

'Fleur, I need to know that you are all right.' She seems detached and worried, as if she is caught up in some dilemma in her mind.

'Of course, Agnes. It's you I'm concerned about.'

'I ask because I am finding it much more challenging now to run my café than I used to. Lately, neither my energy nor enthusiasm has been the constant and reliable companions of old.'

'Agnes, you have been doing this for a long time now, and maybe you should think about selling it.'

'No. What I would appreciate though is some help. I need somebody to take it over and run it. It would allow me to be the gracious and elegant hostess that my reputation has rightly established me to be in the mindsets of my customers.'

I feel a small surge of excitement.

'Fleur, I would be prepared to share the responsibilities with you, if you would consider helping out an old lady, without making it appear so.'

'Agnes, I don't know anything about being responsible for a café.'

'How can you not? You have several years of experience at the Guerbois and I have been hearing all about your gastronomic tours through the city. Think about it. It won't be for at least a month yet, as I will have to let one of the kitchen staff go, but I have already selected Margot as I know she is carrying the child of one of the delivery men. I just have not deduced which one, though I am sure her powers of deduction will be no more accurate than mine.'

She tightens a comb back into her hair, catching up some stray ends.

'My little establishment is in need of a fresher touch I feel. Men like to be flattered by younger women. The younger and prettier, the more their virility is unfurled like a banner from the rooftops for all to bear witness. You handle people with grace and that will always stand you well. Maria can cast her artistic eye over this little place and breathe life, energy and colour into it. This place needs the cantankerous debate of the painters. I do not want to lose their custom which I fear would happen if there is any depletion of my spirit.'

She fixes me with a stare and seems now most present. 'Fleur, I am doing this for me, but I am hoping you will benefit as well. You need to stay strong and focused.' She takes my hand. 'We know we have to hold fast to things, and that this can take a great effort sometimes. Neither of us can be like bobbing corks. We cannot trust ourselves.'

My heart melts for Agnes, but I am concerned that her inclination is to immediately draw me into her parameters. I can be trusted. I know that she can trust me.

It is agreed. Together we can run this café. This vow is consecrated by the haze of the moon as it streams through the lace curtains, making patterns on the wall. It is as if we are in one of the new shadow theatres that are opening up everywhere, where puppets are cut into silhouettes and shown in relief to the audience. At this moment, Agnes looks as fragile as a paper silhouette. We hug each other firmly in an act of defiance to the shadowy tricks of light.

* * *

Maria comes for a walk with me up to the top of the Butte. We sit on the same wall that had been our favourite viewing place only a few years earlier, but a complete lifetime away.

'I expect Maurice will soon be running about these very same streets.'

'Yes, and probably only then will you realise what a hard time you gave your mother.'

'Please God, I'm not finished yet. She's a tough old bird. I'm sure Maurice will go easier on me.'

'You can't afford to be too unkind about her, otherwise she'll hand him over to you and tell you to get on with it.'

'True. Henri was telling me that he showed a couple of my drawings to Degas, who he said was very impressed. If I could get Degas to buy something from me then I could give my mother more money, which would please her no end. People listen to Degas. If he likes my works, then who knows? In fact, I don't care if he buys anything, his approval would be valuable enough. Mistress of a café. You! Fleur! It's so exciting.'

'I don't know if I can do it, Maria.'

'Agnes believes in you completely and that is all you need to know.'

'The Guerbois is not going to be very happy. Or maybe I'm overestimating my value!'

We sit on in silence, swinging our legs in an ankle lock with each other. She pulls her coat tight around her, wincing a little.

'Maurice will be ready for a feed. I'm beginning to leak here.' She slides off the wall and with a quick kiss to my cheek, walks briskly down the hill.

I watch her disappearing into the rough-hewn labyrinth. The dotted gas lamps below make it look as if a carpet of stars has rolled out before me. I can tip-toe through this half-way world, at ease within its margins.

I must tell Walrus. He will be so proud of his apprentice.

* * *

It has been over a week now and there has been no sign of Walrus. I had instructed young Joseph to try to track where he could be found. Joseph had readily agreed, for a small price of course, so it's with huge relief that, as I turn into my street, I can see Joseph sitting on my front step. He stands up with a broad grin.

'It wasn't easy, but that's why I'm the best. He lives near the corner of Rue Laffitte. There's a small butcher's shop, and he lives above it.'

'Above a butcher's shop? That can't be right. Are you sure?'

'Doubt me if you insist, but go see if you can prove me wrong.'

'I didn't mean to … thank you for your help.'

It is still early evening and I know I won't sleep tonight if I do not speak with him and satisfy myself that all is well. I set off. I need his endorsement. I know that he will be truthful with me. I am familiar with Rue Laffitte. Maria has spoken about it many times, crammed as it is with small galleries, dealers and art-supply shops. Unknown painters nudge up against more established artists. Many dealers slip in the work of talented unknowns when mounting an exhibition. She has told me all of this in hushed tones.

It is a narrow street, slightly muddy underfoot, framed at one end by the columns and the dome of the Notre-Dame de Lorrette church looming imposingly, as if in judgment. I find the butcher shop a few doors below a funny little shop that makes and sells candles.

The door is slightly ajar so when I push on it, it easily opens into a small dark hallway. I get a strong smell of what seems to be animal intestines. The staircase has narrow scuffed wooden steps. I pad my way tentatively upwards in a symphony of creaks until I reach the only door on the dusty second-floor landing. I knock, at first gingerly and then loudly and hear the slight shuffling of furniture being pushed aside and the cumbersome sound of someone moving slowly across the floor. Walrus's cheeks flush slightly on seeing me at his door.

'Mademoiselle, what are you doing here?'

Without being prompted to, I cross into the apartment. Walrus slowly closes the door behind me. I am standing immediately in a tiny kitchen area with a short counter and a small stove lined to one side. To my right, an open doorway which leads straight into another slightly bigger room. There is a mattress on a wooden platform placed just under the sloped ceiling, a fireplace with a large mirror resting on it with a few picture postcards tucked into its frame and a cluttered desk to the right of it. Apart from that, there are a couple of hooks for clothes, dozens of books piled high to the ceiling at the foot of the bed, a battered divan and one plump well-used arm chair. Walrus pulls out the chair that is tucked under the desk.

'I'm not used to visitors.'

'I have to say, I'm surprised Monsieur Mitoire. It is not how I expected you to be living.'

He shrugs.

'I became a little worried for your well-being when you didn't show up at the Guerbois for over a week.'

'I've been in a bit of discomfort and unable to walk any great distance. My toe is throbbing and most painful to put pressure on.'

'Let me make you something. Are you hungry? Have you been eating?'

'There is a bottle of Crème de Menthe on the shelf under the basin. Just pull back the curtain and you'll find a couple of glasses too.'

The shelves are pitifully empty. I pour two generous glasses and hand Walrus one as I take my seat again. We clink glasses in some ridiculous nod to civility and take the first two sips in silence. Walrus smoothes his moustache between his thumb and forefinger.

'You are clearly grasping for some kind of explanation.'

I laugh a little. 'Let's just say I would have pictured your household to be a little, eh, grander. You Sir, are clearly a well-bred man with distinguished tastes. I would have expected servants and fine crystal and a heaving larder. I would have imagined your ceiling to be buckling with the weight of a glistening chandelier. You don't even have enough food to rustle up a proper supper.'

'That is the very decent thing about Paris. If you know enough people, you will never be without a meal.'

'Did you lose your fortune somewhere along the way?'

'My dear Mademoiselle, I was never possessed of one. I shall let you into the secret of my true background. From a young boy, I served as a valet at many fine tables, as did my Papa before me. He served the greatest of them all, the father of gastronomy as an art, the passionate Grimod de La Reynière, author of several almanacs. Everything I know about food, dining and etiquette, I pilfered with the surreptitiousness audacity and dexterity of a pick-pocket and believe me, it has served me well.'

We sip again.

'The Revolution caused a scattering. The traditions that were once locked away like trinkets in a cabinet, only available to certain elite, became accessible to all and sundry. Other people's skills, talent and knowledge are like curios and vanities, all there to be purloined.'

'I came to tell you that I have been given the opportunity to help Agnes run her café.'

I look expectantly towards him over the rim of my glass as I sip again.

'That is wonderful. And you are more than ready, thanks to my tutelage.'

That is all I needed to hear. I stand up.

'I plan on doing a little decorating and opening it up in three weeks and I very much hope you will be there.'

'I shall do my very best. That will be the first day of May, an excellent beginning. It brings with it the promise of flavour when herbs are at their best. I look forward to your adventure.'

It would not be the same without the approval of Walrus. I'm glad I found him, but I also hate being responsible for embarrassing him and making him feel in any way ill at ease. I reach for the door latch and hope he doesn't feel judged.

I arrange to have a nice piece of pork sent up from the butcher's shop below him.

Bouquet Garni

My little apartment is infused with the scent of freshly picked flowers that I brought back from home. There are very good reasons why I do not go home more often. I was anxious in the days leading up to my visit and in a state of tension during my whole time there. But the telling thing was the relief that washed through me as the train pulled away to bring me back to Paris. The band that had been tightening around my head each day that I stayed there had already loosened as I took my seat in the carriage.

I felt cheery with my basket of fresh blooms at my feet, especially the jasmine that I picked at night. It seems to keep its sweetness longer that way. My little perfume experiments are paying off. I have been thinking about Fleur and feel she would appreciate a nice gift of scent.

Decanting the scented water through the muslin cloth into a little bottle, I know that I will probably have to give it to George to pass on to Fleur. I am unsure why, but he seems not to be in any hurry to facilitate a meeting between us. I trust that his time spent in her company is because she has been very distressed of late and he is such a good person that this is something he would be unable to ignore. He has been away a lot, but I have been keeping busy with my perfumes. The maid, I can tell, is becoming irritated with the bundles of flowers she is being asked to fetch from the market. Each day, I pummel and grind the petals, then soak them in large bowls overnight, then boil them up, then decant them into bottles. I must surely be scenting up our whole street.

I have had an odd exchange with Philippe. He came to visit, as I am apparently being missed. He thought I looked a little pale. Perhaps I am disinclined to venture out, but he should be pleased that I have been occupying my time so productively. Yes, perhaps I have no need for so many bottles of perfume as I have produced, but I thought him a little over-excitable as he kept opening up doors of cupboards and wardrobes and trunks and finding my bottles. Where else can I store them? Every shelf space is also needed. And I need to keep the flowers soaked until I can use them, so naturally there will be buckets of blooms everywhere too. I would rather not spend my money on nonsensical things such as gloves and hats anymore. George is being punished and ostracised by his family because of me so I am determined not to spend my days in shops. His mother's words blow through my mind like a witch's whistle and I know that I am not good for him, for his future, but if I remain strong and fence everybody else out then our little pasture will be safe.

Philippe accepted a gift of lavender from me and also said that he would give the jasmine to Fleur as he is apparently in some type of communication with her over her mother. He assures me that George is particularly busy at the moment, something he witnessed himself when he went to visit with his nephew, Gaston. There must be a lot on his mind as he tries to somehow secure a future for us. It is probably just as well that he has not visited me lately, as there are several plants that I have tried to hide from him, which I brought back from his mother's garden, not that he would recognise them. Poor George. He is under so much pressure because of me. I do sense that he has become distant from me. My greatest fear is that he will regret the risk he took for me – that one day he will look at me and will be filled with resentment. If it comes to that, he will have lost everything and I will have lost him. Now that I am two bottles down, I must crush some more petals. I must chop up some plants. In my head, his mother's witch's whistle. In my hand, his mother's witches weed.

I have my board out and I am chopping to the voices of Lakmé and her servant, Mallika, singing the 'Flower Duet'. Singing as clearly as if they were standing over my shoulder. But I am simply remembering; '*Sous le dôme épais ou le blanc jasmine. Ah! Descendons, ensembles!*' The datura slices easily under my blade.

JASMINE

Have I enough tarragon? I am not used to measuring with any great precision and I must use my instinct alone. I shall chop up some more. The café looks lovely, so fresh and appealing. I had toyed with various themes when it came to decorating. I thought perhaps of using rich fabrics and colours, like velvet and crimsons and white and gold, or of turning it into a parlour room with lace netting and embroidered table cloths, but opted instead for a light and airy style with seaside colours and wooden chairs painted white and the walls in a soft blue. I hung some heavy fishing nets along one side and decorated them with porcelain starfish that I picked up from a Chinese trader.

I expanded the choice of fish dishes and added salmon in Champagne cooked with crayfish, and *hors d'oeuvres* of herrings and also fish stews. I have kept the kitchen in the same cosy undisturbed warmth that Agnes is used to toiling away in, not wanting to alter it in any way. I spent the afternoon turning jars on the shelves so that they are all facing me, checking the cold storage and the hooks where meat is to be hung, casting my eye over the several baskets of vegetables lined up on the counter.

A special table has been set aside for George and Babette, Maria and Henri and Gaston along with a few spare places. As customers drift in, hanging their hats and coats on discreet wall hooks, Agnes hands out a welcoming drink of claret with Seville oranges, cinnamon, cloves and castor sugar which I prepared earlier. Let me think; the soups and *hors d'oeuvres* have been prepared, while steaks, cutlets and little birds on skewers are sizzling away in the ovens. The sauces have been created for the fish dishes and the quantity of garlic has been checked and re-checked. Agnes has been whipping up pastry all afternoon which is ready for a filling of *crème patisserie*. I can then perfume it with vanilla or chocolate or almonds, depending on the customers' wishes. I feel over-wrought with excitement. This is all so very important to me.

Flitting around the tables while offering polite chatter, I notice the light from the doorway darken slightly and I turn towards it. Walrus ambles through with a walking stick and a wide grin.

I smile, and dip into a little curtsey. 'I am honoured to have you here, Monsieur.'

He takes my hand and kisses it lightly. 'Mademoiselle, I am determined that indigestion will kill me and not some uninspiring accident of fate. Though my toe throbs, my spirit and stomach are willing.'

My head is a little light. It must be the excitement but I suddenly feel ill and without wishing to make a fuss, I slip through the kitchen and out the back door where I sit on a step to take some fresh air.

'Are you quite all right?'

I raise my head and follow the long lines of Dr Philippe's legs. I immediately stand up, dusting off the back of my skirt.

'Yes, yes. Just a little tired. This has been a lot more work than I realised. Have you news of my mother?'

There is a look of concern on his face, which I am becoming very alarmed about. He fumbles first in one pocket, then in another and retrieves something.

'I have a gift for you from Babette.'

Maybe it is what happens to people in the medical profession over time: their countenance petrifies into one that seems to be always on the verge of breaking bad news. A smile must require supreme effort as they are instinctually inclined towards reflecting concern. It is what they see most. Who would intentionally pay them a visit harbouring anything other than a worry about something? They must always remain in a state of readiness for this. I shall therefore excuse his grim demeanour.

I pop open the glass stopper and sniff deeply. It is the sweetest jasmine. It is startling. I sniff again. It is familiar. There is more. It is … I close my eyes and feel a swinging in my head, in my mind.

Swing … it is so familiar. As if swinging in a jasmine-scented breeze, I am back in the hallway, back at the Spanish painter's studio. He is dying and bloodied. I am crouched near his head and can hear the faintest of breaths. Turpentine and blood and jasmine. No, I am now at the top of the stairs. I am holding … I'm not sure what … a cast of a foot perhaps, the kind artists use to sketch. I wipe it with a rag and replace it on a shelf.

* * *

Who are all of these men standing in a circle around me? They look aghast. Some are whispering to each other, others rubbing their chins, some shaking their heads. I am wearing a simple crisp white shirt and a plain grey skirt, nothing that would draw the attention of a group of men. It is like a dour carousel, only it is me who is pivoting in the centre, trying to recognise and interpret these bearded faces. Ah, there is Philippe. Thank God, he will make sense of this for me.

'Fleur?'

I cock my head a little. He looks tired. I think perhaps he needs an outing. Maybe I should suggest another trip to the opera.

'Philippe, don't be silly, it's Lily.'

It is odd how we have maintained this pretence. He knew me as Lily from Madame's house and even though he has long since learned that my name is really Babette, we have kept that little charade going. Maybe it was easier for both of us.

'Babette?'

Oh for heaven's sake, he is in a very confused state today. If he wants to call me Babette, that is perfectly fine.

'Yes, Babette if you like.'

The dour faces collapse into a chain of whispering. I try, through a steely gaze, to flash my annoyance at them. I am not sure if I am hitting enough of my targets.

'Philippe, would you please explain why I am here?'

I have a horrible feeling that he does indeed want me to be Lily, and to introduce me to these men. Maybe, indeed, he wants to pass me on to another benefactor and this is some type of selection process. Or to pass me around them all. How dare he. Surely he has retained some fondness for me even though he is well aware of my feelings for George. I shall simply turn and walk out of here. This is unacceptable.

He is trying to stop me. I hear myself shout.

'Let go of her arm.'

'Whose arm?'

'Leave Babette alone.'

I am so ashamed. I seemed to have shoved Dr Philippe in his chest. He has taken a few steps back and has had to balance himself. What are all these men twittering about? They are like a murder of crows, all lined up on a branch. My head is swirling. A murder … there was indeed a murder.

'Dr Philippe, there was a murder. I must tell you. A man was killed. Must I confess here and now? I killed a man.'

'Fleur? Is that you Fleur? Why would you kill a man?'

'He was hurting Babette. Babette is so beautiful, men were always hurting her, but she would never defend herself, so in a way it was her own fault. Who are all of these people?'

'Colleagues of mine, Fleur.'

I must gesture to Dr Philippe to come closer to me, because it is a confidence I am sharing. He leans his head low so I can talk softly in his ear.

'Her uncle did dreadful things to her when she was a very young girl. You see, I'm good at taking care of people, so I was only trying to help her. I'm not sure that I meant to kill the Spanish painter, or maybe I did. I am so confused. He had to leave Babette alone, but he wouldn't have, unless I stopped him.'

'Fleur, are you quite sure it was you? How do you know?'

'It was the jasmine. We like jasmine. My mother used to collect sprigs of it and place it on our pillow when I was very small. She tried to distance herself, Babette did, from our childhood, by wearing patchouli. It's quite pungent you know. One of us was wearing jasmine the day he was killed. I can smell lavender on you Doctor. It's very pleasant.'

'Yes, Babette made it for me.'

'Doctor.'

'Yes, Fleur?'

'My mother would like to speak with you.'

'Madame Delphy? Madame Delphy, would you like to see me? Here, let me get you a chair.'

'Thank you Doctor. I'm so sorry to trouble you, but I seem to have run out of that ointment you gave me. I think Fleur used more than you instructed her to.'

'That's quite all right, Madame. I can make another appointment for you.'

'That is so kind of you. I am very grateful.'

* * *

I have a new friend in Madame d'Aubrey, who is said to suffer from a nervous disposition. What nonsense! Are we always to trust these doctors here? Madame d'Aubrey has taken up painting with ducks being her subject of choice. However, she always asks their permission first and if she senses their disapproval, she apologises profusely and removes her easel to another part of the pond. I can see the rim of her straw hat bobbing with each determined step as she marches towards me.

'You. You there. I implore you to take Hector and feed him to your most intolerable customer in this new café of yours. Hector is trying to cause mutiny on the pond. They were perfectly happy for me to paint their portraits, but Hector, well he is not a very handsome bird, and I suspect he knows this, so he makes the most unsettling commotion every time I approach.'

'Madame d'Aubrey, you are confusing me with my daughter. It is she who will be running the restaurant. Needlework is where my skills lay.'

'Well, whichever and whomever, I shan't be curtailed by a mutinous duck. Mutiny, I tell you. Mutiny.'

'Duck will undoubtedly be on the menu, Madame d'Aubrey. She will come for him when he least expects it.'

My mind is busy today. Fleur knows what to do with duck.

Duck. Let me think. I could slice it up simply and serve it with a little sauce of Seville orange or I could get hold of some of those new shallow pans where you can cook by the table on a small flame stove. Yes, that would prove interesting for the customer. Walrus will be pleased.

FLORAL BOUQUET

Galerie du Vingtième Siècle
Rue Laffitte
1911

Exhibition
Suzanne Valadon

'Madness' is an unfair word. It didn't sit easily on my friend of so long ago, the very sweet and exceptionally kind Fleur, nor is it a fair way to describe my son, Maurice. My first solo exhibition and I know that Fleur would have loved it. It was what she always presumed for me. It is what she encouraged me towards.

Maurice can brilliantly and instinctively capture the streets and alleys of Montmartre in his drawings. When I look at them, my mind's eye brings me back to nearly three decades ago when two friends tried to survive on our wits and whatever talents we could cultivate. From what I can understand, her mind was derailed as a young girl. She suffered abuse and then losing her baby, well, it all became too much. I have tried to be sensitive to the complex workings of the mind and the spirit, as I realised from when he was a very small boy, that Maurice was possessed of a fractured spirit.

He has been shunted between various family structures as I experimented with rural domesticity and husbands and lovers. It is with complete conviction that I believe we belong to Montmartre. I want him healthy and content, but that seems beyond his reach. He has the potential to be a great artist, but are great artists ever truly content? There can be a fragile beauty in the most disturbed of minds and, if we are fortunate, it leaks out onto canvases and musical instruments and pages and we are all the better for it.

It is the lust for drink that diminishes Maurice. I wish I could find and make safe what it is he is trying to quench. When he falls into fits of violence and gets himself detained and incarcerated, it is only his piss-stained wretchedness that is evident to all who jeer him. I fear that one day, I will be powerless to do anything but watch his gifts flow down one of the drains of his beloved Montmartre and disappear forever.

I could not help Fleur in any way. I did not know that she was even in need of help as it is only Fleur that I knew. She spoke of her mother, but when I visited she was always occupied doing something else. I think that was my first inkling that she had a disquiet nature. Fleur spoke of conversations that we all had, when in truth, her mother was not someone I had ever met.

And there were the absences – long stretches of time when she just disappeared. I came to expect them and to not be surprised by them. She was always so cheerful and caring whenever we met up that it never occurred to me to be concerned. I was probably too self-absorbed. Fleur and I were like climbers on a trellis – one minute we'd be entwined and blooming, then we'd be shooting off to entangle ourselves somewhere else. It was the great Dr Philippe who became intrigued professionally when he happened upon Babette at Madame Delphine's. She was at first a trinket that he merely purchased but then began to realise that she was a fascinating psychological study.

Madame Delphine knew immediately that something was amiss, as she had already been in Babette's life when she was Fleur. The young pregnant girl would have killed herself by throwing herself down some stairs if Delphine had not come across her. At the time, she had told Fleur that she would always be there for her, and that her door would always be open to her. She was both glad and saddened that the young girl did indeed turn up at her door, for she knew that life could not have gone very well for her. She knew that she could once again, offer her a safe haven. Babette did not realise that she had already been rescued by Delphine. Delphine urged the patron of the Guerbois to be patient, and he was. He may well have been familiar with Madame's house, and was happy to oblige.

George's role was a complicated one. Although he liked to pretend otherwise, he was a cog who had merely slipped for a while, only to realign himself back into its proper functional slotting. To be fair, he was fond of Fleur, and then when he saw her with Philippe at the opera, he did not begrudge her an elaborate outing not normally accessible to a young *serveuse*. When she seemed not to recognise him and he was told that she was a courtesan named Lily, all he could see was the potential to make his own name by penning the great nineteenth-century novel – a taut study of the degenerate female mind. It descended into a ridiculously over-blown gothic novel. When that didn't work, however, it veered into a vaguely pornographic novella. Because he could never formally commit to anything for very long, his initial enthusiasm and application soon spilled into another project. Both Fleur and Babette were used in different ways at different times by the doctor and by George. Though George was genuinely fond of Fleur, I think he fell a little in love with Babette.

He is something important in the world of commerce now and married to a cousin, from what I heard. I used to see him during my marriage to Paul, who was a wealthy businessman, and we moved in overlapping social circles. He would always be in the company of one mistress or other. We never spoke of Fleur, or Babette.

Philippe did take advantage of George in that he knew both Fleur and Babette trusted him. The doctor was terribly excited by the new academic explorations into the psychology of what was being called 'multiple personality disorder'. A condition which in previous decades had been dismissed as part of a culture of séances and para-psychology and even of demonic possession, was now being taken seriously, and Philippe had found himself a genuine case study. And as was being suggested within these academic and professional circles, the dissociative disorder seemed to be conditional on some type of emotionally traumatic experience as a young child. The uncle was completely to blame for her subsequent unravelling. I don't know for sure if baby Isobel was his. She could have been and maybe Fleur might have been able to hold it all together if the baby had lived, but once she died, the fissure was permanent.

Philippe wanted George to help him discover which one was the dominant personality. It was a dangerous experiment, as Babette, in her misery, almost poisoned them both. George relished the challenge of teasing out their separate identities. It became so cruel as neither girl was happy.

And what did my friend look like? Not as beautiful as she imagined Babette to be, nor as plain as she presumed Fleur to be. She was lovely and you couldn't but warm to her. She moved between an apartment on the Champs-Élysées and a hovel in Montmartre, between Babette and Fleur. As for her 'mother', she needed a separate entity into which she could siphon off any sickness or weakness or illness. Both Babette and Fleur needed to be strong and resourceful.

I would like to think that Fleur enjoyed the times we spent together, but I believe she was happiest with Walrus. He taught her the simple, unadulterated satisfaction of a lovingly prepared meal and to trust in the healing powers of a pinch of tarragon.

I have been thinking about all of this as I was asked for a few biographical details for my exhibition. I cannot condemn or judge Fleur for living two and three lives at a time, for the reality is I have spent many years trying to do the same myself. I wasted too long trying to play the role of a bourgeois wife, living with my servants in the countryside as my life, my truth, lay camouflaged and stilled. My old mentor Degas would write to me and chastise me for not drawing more. When my dear friend Henri de Toulouse-Lautrec died his lonely drink-deranged death, it left me bereft and grieving. Grieving with loss for him and for what I had allowed myself to become. We were both in our thirties when he died: a difficult age when many things feel unfinished. It took me a dormant decade before I could properly stir myself and to discover the seed of something planted deep within me.

Following my divorce last year, my new family re-shaped and adapted. We are now Maurice, my mother, and my lover André, and even though he is twenty years younger than me, it feels more natural a fit than anyone ever before. We paint together and he has made me aware of a whole new generation of visionaries and talents, who mingle in the same places that I did more than fifteen years ago.

I have nothing but admiration for Fleur. Her world was no more disjointed than mine. I tried to hang on to my friend but when I last visited her over twenty years ago, it was only her mother that I met, contentedly embroidering away in her clean white room with its smell of starch. I left her a bouquet of flowers.

Acknowledgements

Sincere appreciation and gratitude to Ronan Colgan, Beth Amphlett and Stephanie Boner and The History Press Ireland.

To Vanessa O'Loughlin, Denise Blake, Annie Deppe and Imelda Maguire.

And for Suzanne Valadon – Artist and Frontierswoman